## "I can take care of myself," Erin assured Nick.

"Can you?" he asked.

There was something in his tone—a faint challenge—that made Erin grow even more uneasy. She glanced around the darkened hallway. There was no one about. She was completely alone with a man who made her tremble, a man who made her think of moonlight and madness. Of secrets and whispers and promises that could only be told in the dead of the night.

She looked at him, telling herself that she couldn't be feeling this pull, this strange attraction for a man who seemed to embody her deepest fears. Her darkest nightmares.

*What kind of woman would be drawn to the thing that frightened her most?*

**Amanda Stevens** knew at an early age that she wanted to be a writer, and began her first novel at the age of thirteen. While majoring in English at Houston Community College and the University of Houston, she was encouraged to write a romance novel by one of her instructors, who was himself writing a historical. Her first romance was sold to Silhouette Intimate Moments in 1985. Amanda lives in Houston, Texas, with her husband of sixteen years and their five-year-old twins.

# DARK OBSESSION

# AMANDA STEVENS

Published by Silhouette Books

**America's Publisher of Contemporary Romance**

SILHOUETTE BOOKS

ISBN 0-373-51128-0

DARK OBSESSION

Copyright © 1995 by Marilyn Medlock Amann

Visit Silhouette at www.eHarlequin.com

**Printed in U.S.A.**

# PROLOGUE

Drake D'Angelo woke up suddenly, the realization that it was almost dark and he was starving coming upon him. Soon, he comforted himself. Soon he would taste again the sweet red nectar that he had been deprived of for too many years.

He licked his lips in anticipation as he got up and strolled out to his balcony. The soft twilight fell around him, blanketing him with the cool comfort of the approaching night. This was his favorite time, this tenuous moment right after sunset when the world came alive with the darkness, when the night stretched before him like an endless dream. How he had missed it during those eight years when he had lain deep underground, sleeping the sleep of the dead while the wounds that had nearly destroyed him healed.

He hated the dawn. Hated being trapped by the prison of daylight, but he wouldn't think about that now. Not when the darkness was calling to him so strongly. Not when he had been waiting so impatiently for the night.

Not when revenge finally lay within his grasp.

Visions raced before his eyes, and he let himself remember that night eight years ago—a mere moment

in time for one such as he. The heat had been suf-
focating, stinging his eyes and searing his skin as the
inferno raged around him. The flames had licked at
the tattered drapery and rotting floors of his mansion
as the fire consumed everything in its path.

He closed his eyes at the remembered terror. The
agony! The excruciating pain as the fire caught at his
clothing and ate at his flesh. He could still hear Simone's screams as her long, silken hair blazed like a
halo around her glorious face. Within seconds she had
been gone, destroyed, her loveliness nothing but a
memory.

And all because of one man.

His enemy.

An unworthy rival who had thought to destroy him,
but like the legendary phoenix, Drake had risen from
the ashes of death. He had survived the torment. He
had lived to seek his vengeance against the man who
had taken away the one woman who would have been
Drake's mate through eternity. His one great love. He
had waited centuries for her, and now she was gone.

"Simone." He whispered her name agonizingly in
the gathering darkness. There was only one way to
ease the pain of her memory. Only one way to avenge
her loss.

Death.

Each one would make him feel stronger. Would
take the edge off his loneliness. Would give him a
sense of justice in an unjust world.

They would give him a little something to look forward to night after night, he thought, smiling. Each death, each "kill," would torment his nemesis as once the pain had tormented Drake. The kills would take everything away from his rival as Simone had been taken away from Drake. And he had found the perfect way to once and for all destroy his enemy. Nicholas Slade's pathetic little crusade was about to come to an end.

And so he would go out again tonight, in his new identity, to a club where others like him met. A place where he could see but not be seen. A place where the unsuspecting were so easily seduced by the darkness. He would go there because that was where Slade would be.

Tonight his revenge would begin in earnest.

Drake smiled as his hunger sharpened. He could hardly wait. "I'll see you in hell, Slade," he whispered.

# CHAPTER ONE

Detective Nicholas Slade knelt and touched the dead woman's chin. With his fingertip, he tilted her head, glanced at the bruise marring an otherwise flawless cheek, then let his gaze move downward to her neck.

He studied her perfect features in the dim glow cast by a distant street lamp. She was a beautiful woman. Or had been, he corrected himself. Early twenties. Tall. Slender. Long black hair. And even though her eyes were closed, Slade knew they were blue. Deep, dark, soul-piercing blue.

Megan Ramsey had been a knockout. A real heartbreaker.

Abruptly Slade stood. From behind his sunglasses, he gazed down at the corpse, never taking his eyes off the body even when the other detective on the scene came up beside him.

"Orders came down from the top, Slade. We had to call you." There was a trace of resentment in Gabriel Abrams's voice, but Slade ignored it. His involvement over the last eight years with a special task force set up by Commissioner Thomas Delaney had ruffled a lot of feathers within the New York City Police Department, due in large part to the veil of secrecy from under which the group operated.

Code-named the Mission, the task force's primary function was to investigate and eliminate the dark, evil elements that stalked the city's streets—elements that most people thought only existed in their nightmares.

Each member of the Mission had been carefully recruited over the years by Commissioner Delaney because of a special trait, ability or background that made him or her uniquely qualified to serve in the secret organization. The Mission's ranks expanded far beyond the New York City Police Department, though. Slade had no idea who all the members were or where they had come from. He only knew what his own particular area of expertise was. And why.

"You did the right thing," he told Gabe. "Anyone else know about this?"

"Just the two blues who were on the scene first." Gabe's breath frosted in the night air as he gazed down at the body. "Her name's Megan Ramsey. An actress. We got a positive ID from her sister."

It would have been the perfect time to mention he already knew the victim's name. It would have been the logical time to admit that he had seen Megan Ramsey just last night, that he had warned her to stay away from a club that attracted the dark side of the city, but he didn't. Like so many others, she had refused to listen to him, and now she lay dead at his feet.

Slade shoved his hands deep inside the pockets of his long black coat. "Any witnesses?"

"None that bothered to stick around."

Thank God for small favors, Slade thought. If the citizens of this city had even an inkling as to the real terrors out there in the darkness—

He cut off his own thoughts as he nodded toward a stooped figure in a tan overcoat hovering around the fringes of the cordoned-off area. "Who's the old guy?"

"Name's Traymore. Dr. Leonard Traymore. He's a retired archaeologist doing some kind of research at NYU. He was a little vague on exactly what, though," Gabe said dryly. "Says he heard a commotion and came out to investigate. He's the one who called the station, but he claims he didn't see a thing." Gabe hesitated, then said in a low, anxious tone, "What the hell's going on here, Slade?"

"What do you mean?"

Gabe stamped his feet, trying to keep warm as the wind sharpened. "Look at those marks on her neck. They look like some kind of a bite, but there's no blood anywhere. No sign of a struggle."

Slade stared at Gabe from behind his sunglasses. "So what are you saying, Abrams? That we've got a crazed vampire on the loose?"

"Hell, no. I'm saying we may have some crazed psycho on the loose who *thinks* he's a vampire. Eighty-seventh had a werewolf last year, remember?

Four bodies ripped apart in the park before the perp was apprehended. And the year before that, it was human sacrifices down by the river. The world is full of crazies, Slade. This guy's a real Looney Tunes.''

"What makes you so sure it's a man?'' Slade asked quietly.

Gabe looked startled, then grinned irreverently. "I've met some bloodsucking women in my time— my ex-wife included—but nothing like this. No. This is a man's job. Some crazy bastard getting his jollies. And by the looks of her, she didn't put up much of a fuss.''

Slade stared down at Megan Ramsey, seeing again the perfect, flawless creature at his feet. She wore a black beaded evening dress and silk stockings. One of her shoes had come off and lay several inches from the body. Leaves dotted her dark hair as artfully as if she'd arranged them there herself. The black lashes showed starkly against her white cheekbones, and her full red lips curved upward in a tiny secretive smile. If possible, she looked even more beautiful in death.

A shudder ripped through Slade. He could almost hear the echo of Megan Ramsey's laughter in the wind. Or was that Simone's? *Kiss me, Nick. Just one last kiss...*

"Has anyone else said anything about the marks on her neck?'' he abruptly asked Gabe.

"I don't think so. The blues were too busy admiring her body. They're used to winos and druggies who, shall we say, have already passed their prime when the Grim Reaper comes to call. They don't get to see too many corpses that look like her.''

"What a shame,'' Slade remarked sarcastically. He raked his fingers through his short crop of hair, then looked around, uneasy. It was getting colder. Colder and foggier. In the distance, a siren sounded, but the tiny plot of backyard where they stood remained eerily silent. Deadly calm. Mist swirled over the beautiful corpse like a gossamer shroud.

"The sister's still hanging around if you want to talk to her,'' Gabe suggested, nodding toward the steps of the apartment building. "She's been here the whole time.''

Slade had noticed the woman sitting on the back steps the moment he'd arrived. She wore jeans and some sort of flimsy-looking sweater, and he could see her shivering from cold and shock. She looked fragile, like a crystal figurine that could too easily be shattered.

He tried to look away, but his gaze kept going back to her. The way she sat there, with her shoulders slumped and her hand clutching something to her chest, she looked so forlorn. So lost. Even from the distance across the yard, he could sense her grief, could almost touch it in the air between them. Like a dark and heavy cloak, it settled over them both, drawing them closer, binding them together against his will.

"Her name's Erin," Gabe was saying. "Erin Ramsey."

Slade glanced up sharply. "The horror writer?"

"Apparently. She's the one who discovered the body. Just got in about an hour ago from L.A. Came looking for her sister and found her out here, like this. Some welcome party, huh?"

"Have you talked to her?"

"Briefly. She wasn't in much shape to answer questions."

"Yeah, well, unfortunately, she doesn't have a choice."

"Why don't you do it?" Gabe suggested, eyeing him slyly. "You always have such a charming bedside manner, Slade. I'll talk to the old guy."

Slade nodded, then glanced around, letting his shielded gaze roam over the backyard. The two officers were still hanging around, shuffling their feet and trying not to stare at the body. The medical examiner would be here soon, the CSU team, someone from the D.A.'s office. The yard would become a circus, and what he and Gabe had found wouldn't be a secret for long.

Then what?

He could already feel the heat coming down from the commissioner's office. *This is your province, Nick. Your specialty. Hunt him down, quickly, before questions begin to surface. We can't have a vampire preying on innocent young women. Do what you have to do, but get him off the streets.''*

Yeah, this was his province, all right, and Slade had every intention of doing what he had to do to stop the killing. After all, as the commissioner liked to remind him, vampires were his specialty.

He glanced at the sky and saw that the darkness had lightened almost imperceptibly. Behind the sunglasses, his eyes burned slightly with warning. It would be daybreak in a few hours. So much to do and so little time.

With an inward sigh, he headed across the yard toward Erin Ramsey.

He came toward her out of the mist, moving like a shadow, gliding with the darkness as though he were somehow a part of it. A breeze caught the hem of his long black coat and blew it back, so that it trailed behind him like wings made of leather. He looked huge—tall and broad shouldered, with dark hair cut very short, in blatant disregard for the latest fashion.

But what caught Erin's attention, what held her gaze in fascination was the fact that he wore sunglasses—at night. The yard was dark and misty, but he hadn't once removed his sunglasses since he'd arrived.

A chill of apprehension crept up Erin's spine as he stopped before her. She'd seen the way the other police officers had deferred to him, subtly keeping their distance as they filled him in on the details of the crime.

Now she understood why.

Erin could feel his stare, as keen as a razor, but because she couldn't see his eyes, the sensation unnerved her even more, made her want to run and hide from this man who looked very much like a phantom from her imagination—or her nightmares.

"I'm Detective Slade." His voice was like liquid—not warm and comforting, but cold and smooth, like an icy stream in the dead of winter. Erin shivered, wishing she had her coat. "I'm very sorry about your sister. I understand you were the one who found the body."

He propped a booted foot on the bottom step and leaned forward so she didn't have to look up very far to see him. Strangely, his features stood out prominently in the darkness. She could see him clearly, the well-defined angles of his handsome face, the nose that was a little broad but well shaped, lips that were full and sensuous but unsmiling. His cheeks were roughened with stubble, giving him a dangerous, almost sinister quality. He looked pale in the moonlight, but somehow undiminished, somehow vitally alive.

Erin shivered again and looked away, clutching the silver cross more tightly in her hand. *Too late,* her mind screamed over and over. *Too late, too late, too late.* Why hadn't she come sooner? Why hadn't she been here when Megan had needed her the most? Why hadn't she sensed something was terribly, terribly wrong?

She had. She *had* sensed it. She just hadn't wanted to believe it. Hadn't wanted to be lured back here, to this city, to this very apartment, where her nightmares had first begun.

Erin felt something touch her shoulders, wrap around her gently, like an embrace. He'd removed his leather coat and tucked it around her, and she thought how strange that he would be the one to perform such an act of kindness. He seemed so distant, so emotionless, but perhaps that was the way he handled his job. He probably saw bodies every day.

But not her sister's body. He didn't see her sister's body every day.

Trembling, Erin wrapped the coat more tightly around her shoulders. Detective Slade stared down at her with his protected gaze and said, "Would you like to go inside? We can talk there."

"I can't," she whispered. "I can't leave her."

"You can't help her now," he said, not unkindly. "You'll only make yourself sick if you stay out here."

"When will they take her away?"

"In a little while. The CSU guys have to get here, and someone from the M.E.'s office—" At her blank look he stopped and clarified. "Crime Scene Unit and someone from the medical examiner's office. You don't want to be here for that."

"I'm not leaving." Erin knew she sounded obstinate, but she couldn't help it. There was no way she could leave Megan again. Not until she absolutely had to. "Where will they take her?"

"The morgue."

"Will there be an autopsy?"

Slade hesitated, as if weighing how much more she needed to know. Then he nodded and said, "Yeah" in that same cold, expressionless tone.

Their eyes met in the dark—hers exposed, vulnerable; his hidden, masked. But Erin had no doubt that he was looking at her. She could feel the power of his gaze all the way through her, and it made her shiver all the more deeply.

The wind picked up and tossed a dead leaf across the sidewalk in front of them. Erin stared at it, saw it swirl across the yard toward her sister's body and settle against the silent form. For just an instant, the leaf clung to Megan's stilled body. Then, on a fresh gust of wind, it blew away, lost in the darkness like her sister's soul.

I want to cry, Erin thought. I want to cry so that I'll know I can still feel. But the tears wouldn't come. The tears had all been used up long, long ago on cold, dark, terrifying nights such as this one.

She tried to tell herself that at least now Megan was finally at peace, but when Erin thought of death, she could only think of darkness, eternal night. That was what hell was, she thought. Not fire and brimstone. Just cold, mind-numbing blackness.

Detective Slade settled his long frame on the step beside her. He wore jeans, she noticed. Very faded and very tight. His dark sweater blended with the night and his black boots were trimmed with silver. The dark glasses made him appear aloof and mysterious. Dangerous.

He didn't look like a cop at all. He looked more like a demon. A demon lover she'd conjured up from the deepest recesses of her black imagination.

Erin realized she was verging on hysteria, focusing on the man beside her so she wouldn't have to think or feel or remember. She wanted to forget, even for just a second, that her sister was dead.

With something of a shock, Erin felt the cold moisture streaming down her face. So there were tears left, after all. She put her hands to her cheeks, trying to stem the flow, but more and more came, like backwater seeping through floodgates.

"Let's go inside." The deep voice spoke beside her. She felt his hand on her elbow, felt herself being propelled upward as if by sheer force of will. Suddenly she had no strength to resist. More people had arrived on the scene. They were all standing around or kneeling beside Megan's body, and Erin couldn't stand it. She wanted to scream at them to go away, to leave her sister alone as she had done years ago when the monsters had threatened them both.

But it was too late, she thought sadly. Too late now for anything but remorse.

Without looking back, Erin turned and allowed Detective Slade to lead her up the steps and into the gloomy hallway of her sister's apartment building.

# CHAPTER TWO

The apartment was dark. Erin reached inside the door and flipped on the switch. Bright light spilled into the hallway, and she saw Detective Slade flinch.

"When did you first get here?" he asked with a grim edge to his voice.

"About two hours ago."

He strode past her, and Erin felt the hair at the back of her neck rise as his arm brushed against hers. There was something so unsettling about his touch, something so daunting about his presence in her sister's apartment.

He walked slowly around the room, not touching anything, but Erin had the distinct impression that nothing missed his scrutiny. He paused beside a vase of wilted roses. One fingertip stroked a shriveled petal as he frowned pensively. Then his gaze returned to her, and Erin's heart began to thump inside her chest.

"How'd you get in?" His voice—that deep, cold, spine-tingling voice—shattered the illusion of calm in Megan's apartment.

"I have a key," she told him. "I let myself in. Megan wasn't here. I thought perhaps she'd gotten bored waiting for me and gone out for a while. I was supposed to have been here hours ago, you see, but the flight was late leaving Los Angeles. It was after midnight when we landed at La Guardia. Then I had to get my luggage and find a taxi, and even at that time of night, traffic was horrendous. It took forever to get here...." She trailed off, glancing away as if realizing she'd revealed more than she'd meant to.

So the guilt had already set in. Slade pitied her for that. He'd lived with that same emotion for eight long years, knew how deadly and destructive it could be. He took her arm and steered her toward the couch.

"How did you happen to go out into the yard?" he asked her as they sat down.

"I heard voices. I think I must have dozed here on the couch for a little while. I thought I was dreaming at first. Then I opened my eyes and realized I was awake and the voices were coming from below. The window was open."

She tilted her head toward the French doors that flanked one side of the fireplace. Her black hair, pulled smoothly back and knotted, rippled with iridescence in the light. Her skin was as pale and soft as moonlight, her features delicate, almost fragile.

But her eyes...her eyes were the contradiction. In their violet blue depths, he glimpsed the soul of a woman who could write novels so terrifying that they sent shivers along *his* spine.

She might be in shock now, but Slade knew she wouldn't accept a simple explanation for her sister's murder and then allow herself to go quietly away.

Instinctively he could tell that she would want it all. Every last detail. Her guilt would demand it. He just hoped to God she'd be able to live with the facts when she learned them. *If* she learned them. He would do his damnedest to see that she didn't. That was his job.

Abruptly he got up and walked over to the window. He knelt and examined the latch. "Did you leave the door open?"

"No. It must have been that way when I came in. The latch on that door sometimes sticks. You think it's fastened, but it's not. It's always been that way."

Slade glanced up. "You've been here before then?"

Something flickered in her eyes and then disappeared, but Slade thought again of the horrifying stories she so aptly created. "I lived here as a child," she explained quietly. "My sister and I own this apartment. We grew up here. Megan probably didn't get the lock fixed because...she wanted to prove she wasn't afraid of the dark anymore."

"Lots of things in the dark to be afraid of," Slade murmured. He stepped out onto the balcony and looked down at the yard. The body had already been placed in a bag, but there were still several people milling around in the yard. One of the officers laughed. The sound carried easily to the balcony. Slade glanced back inside, glad suddenly that he'd persuaded Erin to leave the scene below.

"So you heard voices," he said, walking back into the apartment and closing the door to block the sounds from the yard. "Did you recognize them?"

Erin looked up at him. "I thought I heard Megan's voice. I thought I heard her...laughing."

A chill seeped through Slade's skin, accompanied by a cold, dark suspicion. "Did you recognize anyone else?"

Erin shook her head, wrapping his leather coat more tightly around her shoulders. "I think I heard a man's voice, but I'm not sure. It was more like a...like a whisper, and yet I could hear it all the way up here. When I looked out the window, all I could see were shadows. I called to Megan, and I heard her laugh again. That's when I went down to the yard to find her."

"What did you see when you got there?"

She gazed at him reproachfully as if to say, *the same thing you saw, Detective.* But he hoped she hadn't. He hoped to hell she hadn't seen the same thing he had.

Her bottom lip trembled with emotion and she bit it. Slade could almost taste the blood on her tongue. He took a few steps toward her. "What did you see, Erin?"

The sound of her name seemed to startle her. She stared at him as if seeing him for the first time. He moved to the couch and sat down beside her again. The warmth of her presence filled the emptiness inside his soul, and for the first time in eight years, Slade felt a yearning deep inside him. She looked so vulnerable, so…innocent, but he suspected in reality she was neither. And somehow that notion excited him even more.

Back off, he warned himself. She's not for you. But at the moment, all he wanted to do was wrap his arms around her slender shoulders, draw her close to him and protect her from the evil that lurked in the darkness.

The evil that was part of himself.

Erin's eyes widened as if she recognized the danger. Her fingers wrapped around the silver cross that hung around her neck. "I saw Megan lying on the ground," she said. "And I saw…something in the darkness."

Slade's heart jumped into his throat as he stared at her. "Are you saying you *saw* the murderer?"

"I'm not sure what I saw. I didn't see a face, no definite form, but there were these…eyes. Silver eyes. And they were…glowing in the dark.…" Her words trailed away as she met Slade's stare. She couldn't seem to take her eyes off his dark glasses. For endless seconds, their gazes clung. Slade's pulse quickened as he recognized something in Erin Ramsey that scraped along his nerves and left him oddly shaken.

Then the doorbell sounded, breaking the spell, and Erin started to get up. Slade's hand shot out and touched her arm briefly. Her gaze dropped to his hand as if she'd felt the same tiny jolt he had. He heard her gasp softly when she saw the scars. Her gaze flew back up to meet his, and he let his hand fall away from her.

"What else did you see?" he demanded.

"Nothing," she whispered. "That was all."

But that was enough, Slade thought grimly. In fact, too damned much.

Erin Ramsey had seen silver eyes glowing in the dark.

Erin's hands trembled as she crossed the room to answer the door. She didn't like to admit that Detective Slade had left her so shaken, so uncertain of her own emotions. She'd never met a man quite like him before.

But, of course, she'd just found her sister—her only family—dead in the backyard. Erin suspected she was still in shock. No doubt that was why Detective Slade had affected her so strangely.

Trying to summon the last vestiges of her courage, she drew open the front door. A woman she had never seen before stood on the other side.

"You must be Erin," the woman said. "I came just as soon as I heard." She was tall, towering over Erin by several inches, and she had the most extraordinary red hair Erin had ever seen. It flowed down her back, almost to her waist, and even in the dim hallway light, the thick ringlets blazed with fire. She was dressed all in black—tight leggings, a loose knit sweater and high leather boots. She hovered on the threshold as if waiting for Erin to invite her inside.

Erin said, "I'm sorry, but I'm afraid I don't know who you are."

"My name is Racine DiMeneci," the redhead said. "I live downstairs. I saw Dr. Traymore in the hallway. He told me what happened." Tears filled the woman's green eyes. "I talked to Megan just a few hours ago and now...I can't believe...she's gone...."

"Won't you come in?" Erin said, opening the door wider so the woman could enter.

"I won't stay long," Racine promised, unobtrusively blotting the corners of her eyes with a lace hankie as she stepped inside. "I just had to tell you how sorry I am. If there's anything at all I can do—" She broke off when she saw Detective Slade.

He was standing near the fireplace, watching them with the same shuttered scrutiny that had unsettled Erin earlier. He was holding one of the pictures Megan had kept displayed on the mantel, but as Racine and Erin entered the room, he turned and set it down with hardly more than a glance.

Racine looked back at Erin. "I don't mean to intrude. I probably should have called first, but I hated to think of you being up here all alone. It must have been such a horrible shock. I still can't believe it myself...." Her words trailed away again as she glanced back at Detective Slade.

Erin wondered what his reaction would be to such an overtly beautiful woman, but she could tell nothing by his expression. Slowly he walked toward them, and even Racine seemed intimidated by his formidable appearance.

"I'm Detective Slade," he said.

Racine's gaze flickered with uncertainty as if she didn't quite believe him. "Do...I know you from somewhere?" she asked almost reluctantly, almost fearfully.

"Not likely," he said tonelessly. "How well did you know Megan Ramsey?"

"We were friends." Racine's green eyes filled with tears again. She dropped down onto the couch, her legs crumpling. Erin sat beside her, and Racine reached for her hand, clutching it in her own. The intimacy of the action startled Erin. She wanted to draw her hand back. She wasn't used to closeness, to this easy familiarity. She wasn't used to friendships of any kind, but Racine seemed oblivious to Erin's discomfort.

Detective Slade remained standing, gazing down at them from behind those mysterious glasses. "When was the last time you saw her alive?"

"Last night. Megan had the lead role in a play at the Alucard Theater, and the director, Roman Gerard, had been spending a lot of extra time, you know, coaching her. But there wasn't a rehearsal last night so she came home early, around nine, I think. We spoke for a few minutes, then she said she was going to change her clothes and go back out to meet a friend.''

"Do you know who?"

Racine shrugged. "She didn't say, but I assumed it was someone from the play. There's this nightclub down by the river where a lot of actresses and actors hang out. I don't recall the name of it, but the outside is painted black and the windows are all boarded up, you know, as if it's deserted or something.''

"I know the one you mean," Slade said. "Did you ever go there with her?"

"A couple of times." Racine hesitated. A strange darkness passed across her features, a mere flicker, but it left Erin with a vague feeling of unease, a nagging little worry that there were more things in this room left unspoken than were being revealed.

Racine's gaze met Erin's, then she glanced away. She took a deep, shuddering breath and said, "Lately, Megan seemed to go there quite a lot. At first she said it helped her to understand the character she was portraying in the play. Then later, I think...I think she became obsessed with that club and with things that were, you know...not quite normal...."

"What do you mean?" Erin asked quickly.

"The supernatural," Racine said, avoiding Erin's gaze. "People go to that club pretending to be... vampires."

An eerie chill stole up Erin's spine. "Are you saying that Megan went there because she believed in vampires?'' A memory of the last conversation she'd had with her sister flashed through Erin's mind. Megan had seemed fascinated by *Demon Lover,* Erin's latest novel. She'd asked Erin countless questions about her research for the book, but at the time Erin had given it little thought. It wasn't until later, when she'd begun to suspect her sister was in trouble, that Erin had thought back on their conversation. She could hear Megan's voice now, as clearly as if she stood in the room with her.

"Do you believe in vampires, Erin?"

Erin's own response had been automatic. "Of course not. *Demon Lover* came from my imagination, Megan. He doesn't exist."

"But what if he does?" Megan had insisted.

As the dialogue floated through her mind, Erin's gaze moved upward, almost against her will, to Detective Slade. Even though she couldn't see his eyes, she knew his gaze was on her, as well, and she felt an almost physical jolt.

His mouth had tightened into a grim line, giving his face an even harsher, more formidable appearance. Abruptly he reached past her and picked up his coat. His hand skimmed her arm, and a dangerous shiver sliced through Erin.

"Someone will be talking to you again later today," he said. "We'll need statements, but I won't trouble you anymore tonight. In the meantime, I advise you both to exercise caution. Don't go out alone after dark. Don't open your door to strangers and don't invite anyone inside. We're dealing with a murderer here. A vicious monster who is still out there somewhere. Until he's caught, no one is safe. And I mean *no one.*''

He'd addressed the warning to both of them, but Erin sensed that he was staring at her. How disconcerting, how very frustrating not be able to see his eyes. What was he thinking? Was this just another routine case to him? Would he walk out that door and forget all about Megan? Would he forget Erin? Somehow the notion left her feeling bereft. His presence dominated the room, and now that he was making preparations to leave, the apartment seemed empty already. Lonely. Forbidding. Frightening.

The nightmares were closing in again.

Erin followed him to the door as he shrugged into his coat. The collar was turned up, shading the lower part of his face. The dark glasses hid the rest. She might have been looking at a mask.

She reached for the knob just as he did. Briefly his fingers closed over hers. His hands were huge and strong-looking—not cool and smooth like Racine's, but warm, vital, competent hands. Even the scars—those horrible scars—seemed to give him an air of permanence, of immortality. He had been burned, she thought. Badly. But he had managed to survive.

And now Erin had a sudden, chilling premonition

that her life had been placed in those battered hands. The feeling was oddly comforting. And frightening.

As if reading her thoughts, he said in his dark, liquid voice, "I'll be in touch."

And somehow Erin knew he would be.

"Detective Slade? May I have a word with you?"

Slade slowed his steps as the old man appeared out of the shadows in the backyard. "Dr. Traymore, isn't it?"

"At your service," he said with a slight inclination of his head. There was something old-worldly about the way the man dressed, the way he talked. Slade had a strange feeling of foreboding as he stared at him. "I take it you've questioned Miss Ramsey?"

Slade nodded absently. Yes, he'd questioned her. He'd lingered far longer than he should have. The moment he'd set eyes on Erin Ramsey, Slade had known she was going to be trouble. She would want answers, and Slade suspected she wouldn't rest until she had them. And what would she do when she found out he'd known her sister? Where would she take the information?

He'd been through an investigation once, years ago. He didn't care to repeat the process. One way or another Erin Ramsey would have to be satisfied, before her suspicions could be aroused.

With an effort, Slade shrugged off his growing dread of the days to come, letting his gaze roam the backyard, automatically focusing on the crime scene. The CSU team had finished their preliminary work, and the body was en route to the morgue. The only thing to indicate the violence that had taken place earlier was the yellow ribbon that still cordoned off the area. By morning, it would most likely be gone, as well. He returned his gaze to Dr. Traymore. "I presume Detective Abrams has spoken with you already?"

"Oh, yes. He questioned me thoroughly. I'm to come down to your station later today to make an official statement. I'll tell you everything, Detective Slade, no need to be concerned about that. But I'd like to ask you a question now, if I may."

"What is it?"

"Who did this?" Traymore made a vague gesture with his hand toward the yard. "Or should I say 'what'?"

"If I knew that, I wouldn't be standing here talking to you, now would I?"

"I think you have clues," the old man insisted. He took a pipe from his overcoat pocket and busied himself filling the bowl. "I think you know exactly what you are dealing with here. This is not the work of a psychopath, a 'Looney Tunes' as your colleague so eloquently put it. Something far more dangerous is at work here. An animal who hunts the night. A predator who is voraciously hungry. A creature who is diabolically evil. You and I both know there will be more killings before this is over, Detective Slade.''

A gust of wind swept through the trees overhead and blew down Slade's collar. A chill crawled through him as he stared at the old man's careworn face. The hazel eyes returned his regard without wavering. Dr. Traymore seemed to be looking through the dark lenses of Slade's glasses, straight through his eyes into his soul. Slade suppressed a shudder. "Who are you?" he asked coldly. "What do you want?"

"I'm many things," the old man evaded. "A scholar. An archaeologist. A man who has traveled the world searching for answers. I think you can give me those answers, Detective Slade."

"I'm just a cop," Slade said, "and if anyone's going to be asking questions around here, it's me."

"You're more than a cop, as we both know."

"And you're wasting my time. I've got an investigation to conduct, so if you'll excuse me..." Slade brushed past Dr. Traymore and started across the yard.

"Does the word *nosferatu* mean anything to you, Detective Slade?"

Slade stopped. The whole world seemed to stop. He could feel his heart pounding inside his chest as he turned slowly to face Dr. Traymore. Fog curled around the old man's head like a misty blue halo.

He smiled. "I thought that would get your attention." He walked through the light drizzle toward

Slade. "You see, I've known of the existence of these creatures for a long time."

"You've been reading too many Stephen King novels," Slade said. "Or Erin Ramsey novels," he added with irony.

The old man chuckled as he shoved one hand into the pocket of his heavy overcoat. "I assure you, the books I've been reading are not modern-day fiction. They are hundreds of years old, written in German and Russian, as well as Latin and ancient Greek. I've even seen hieroglyphs in the Valley of the Kings that depict the rising of the undead to feast on human blood. For years I've studied the mysteries of the undead. I've learned their habits. I know what they must have in order to survive. I know their needs and their strengths and their weaknesses. I even know what it takes to kill them."

"Go home," Slade ordered, frustrated that yet a new problem had presented itself to him. It was another worry that would have to be taken care of. "Obviously you need your rest."

Traymore shook his head. "You don't fool me, Detective. I know you're worried. We both are, because if I'm right and certain precautions aren't taken, Megan Ramsey could come back. And if that happens, her sister will be in a great deal of danger."

Almost reluctantly, Slade's gaze lifted to the window of Megan Ramsey's apartment. Framed by the light, Erin stood there, her eyes—those deep, blue eyes—reflecting, not shock any longer, but fear, as if she somehow *knew*. As if she was standing there, watching and waiting for what was to come.

A finger of dread slid down Slade's spine. When would it all end? he thought. How many more people would have to die before the evil could be stopped?

Erin stood looking out the window, gazing down at the exact spot where Megan's body had lain. She saw Detective Slade talking to the old gentleman who had called the police for her earlier, and as she stood looking down at them, Slade's head lifted and he seemed to be gazing directly at her.

Erin gripped the cross hanging from her neck, automatically seeking protection as she felt fear stirring within her. For the first time since she'd found Megan's body, it hit her just how alone she was now. Deeply alone. Terrifyingly alone. There was no one she could turn to for help.

Dr. Traymore walked away, and for what seemed like an eternity, Erin stood staring down at Detective Slade, their gazes locked in a silent communication that seemed fostered by the darkness. Then suddenly, almost angrily, he turned and melted into the darkness.

Shaken, Erin turned from the window and began to pace the apartment. She should have felt better, knowing Detective Slade was out there in the darkness, but somehow she didn't. Somehow his presence disturbed her more than she cared to admit. What was it about him that drew her, in spite of her grief? What was it about him that intrigued her, in spite of her distrust?

What was it about him that made her want what she had always feared the most?

Erin clung to her cross as her pacing accelerated. It was late, nearly dawn, and she knew she should try to get some sleep as the coming days and nights would be trying enough. But in spite of her exhausted state, sleep was the last thing she wanted.

After all these years it was hard enough just being back here in this apartment. More difficult still to think about going into her sister's bedroom, lying in her sister's bed, falling asleep perhaps to dream her sister's dreams.

Dreams that were also Erin's. Nightmares that had belonged to both her and Megan since they'd been abandoned all those years ago.

Erin crossed the room to examine one of the pictures on the mantel—the one Detective Slade had been holding earlier. She tried to imagine what he'd seen when he'd looked at the faces of the two little girls. Innocence? A lovely thought, but Erin saw beyond the ribbons and lace, the white gloves and straw hats. She saw sad smiles and haunted eyes. Terrified hearts and agonized souls.

Kneeling behind the two little girls was their mother, a beautiful young woman who had had cold blue eyes and an even colder heart. Desiree, she'd called herself. It wasn't until years later that Erin had learned her mother's real name was Doris. Doris Ramsey, a sometime actress, who had discarded her name as easily as she'd discarded her children.

If Erin closed her eyes, if she concentrated hard enough, she could still conjure up her mother's made-up face, could almost smell her cloying perfume as she bent to place cool lips against her daughters' cheeks. Erin could hear the whispery voice that still raised chill bumps along her spine, even in memory.

"Erin, I'm counting on you to take care of your sister. Don't open the door to any strangers. And whatever you do, don't let anyone inside, no matter what they say. It could be one of the monsters, tricking you. Remember that."

Night after night, after Desiree had gone out, the two little girls had sat all alone in the apartment, watching the shadows on the walls, listening to the wind outside and waiting for the monsters to come and get them.

Erin had been four years older than Megan, and Megan had depended on her to chase away the nightmares, to stare down the unseen terrors, to scream at the demons to go away.

Now it was too late. Too late for Erin to chase away Megan's monsters. The only thing she could ever do for her sister now was to find the one who had killed her. Somehow that thought comforted Erin, gave her a purpose that made her feel stronger. She gazed around the apartment, the place where the nightmares had started. After all these years, maybe this was the place to finally put them to rest. To face down those monsters once and for all and make them go away.

But in spite of her resolve, when Erin finally fell asleep on the couch, her rest was plagued with distorted visions of dark creatures and laughing demons and Megan calling to her for help. Wearing her black beaded dress, Megan stood outside the French doors in the living room, her face pale and drawn, her eyes rimmed with darkness as her long, inky hair streamed back from her face. She lifted her hand and beckoned to Erin. "I'm so alone and frightened," she whispered. "So cold. Open the door and let me come in, sissy."

And then an ominous voice whispered in Erin's ear, "Whatever you do, don't invite anyone inside." Erin whirled and saw Detective Slade appear out of the darkness. His black leather coat trailed behind him as he moved through the mist toward her.

"But she's my sister!" Erin cried.

Detective Slade smiled, but his eyes were completely hidden by his dark glasses. "Trust me, Erin. You must trust me."

"I can't! I can't trust anyone!"

"Then you'll never be free of the monsters." He retreated into the blackness and vanished before her very eyes. She spun back to the window, but Megan had already disappeared, too.

And Erin was all alone.

She woke up crying. Shivering violently, she lay huddled on the couch, watching the patterns on the ceiling shift and change like stones in a giant kaleidoscope. Just images, she told herself. Just nightmares.

*We've been waiting for you, Erin,* the wind moaned outside.

"You won't get me," Erin whispered. "You don't exist." But her hands were trembling as she clutched the silver cross to her heart.

# CHAPTER THREE

Erin was amazed at how quickly the autopsy was performed and the body released to her for burial. She saw no reason to delay. After all, there was no other family to be considered, just her. With Detective Slade's help and encouragement, the simple memorial services were hastily arranged and conducted late that afternoon.

It was a perfect day for a funeral, overcast and cold, with sharp gusts of wind, which tugged at the hem of Erin's white wool coat. By the time the small procession arrived at the cemetery, the rain had come. The sky grew ever blacker, more threatening, flapping the black canvas awning covering the grave like the wings of a giant bat.

Erin stood at the edge of the open grave and wished she was anywhere but here. She'd written about funerals. Dozens. Usually it was the heroine's mother she had buried in her books. But never the sister. Never had Erin imagined what it would be like to bury her own sister.

Cold and shivering, she watched as Father Grady said the final prayer, then tossed a handful of dirt into the grave. He motioned to Erin, and she stepped forward. Unfastening her necklace, she dropped it into the grave.

The silver cross seemed to glow with an ethereal light as it lay atop the ebony coffin. It was the last thing—the only thing—Erin could give to her sister to thwart the darkness that had tormented them both for years. Megan needed it more than Erin did now, but as Erin stood at the edge of the grave, an almost overwhelming sense of foreboding stole over her.

As if drawn by a magnet, she turned her head and glanced over her shoulder. Through the misty veil of rain, she saw a male figure dressed all in black standing at the edge of the cemetery as if hovering on the threshold of a room he was forbidden to enter.

The form seemed to waver in the drizzle while the mist swirled around him with an unnatural movement. Erin couldn't see a face, but somehow his dark gaze penetrated the layers of fog as easily as a beam of concentrated light. There was something familiar about the apparition, she thought. Something... dangerous.

Something evil.

Erin began to shake. She struggled to look away, but his dark gaze held her imprisoned. A strange lethargy crept over her. She tried to fight it, but slowly Erin felt herself drifting away, floating on a mystical cloud that seemed to carry her to this menacing stranger. She heard a voice, a dark, persuasive voice borne by the wind. *We've been waiting for you,* it whispered. *Your sister's here, Erin. I can take you to her. Don't let her down this time.*

A wave of dizziness washed over Erin, and a blackness so cold and so swift it seemed as if icy waters were closing over her head. She felt herself sway, and then her knees began to buckle. She was falling, plunging toward Megan's open grave, descending toward that yawning abyss, that dark place from which there would be no return....

*Erin! Help me!*

Was that Megan's voice that called to her? Was that Megan's cry she heard?

Suddenly Erin no longer had the will to fight. She closed her eyes and let the darkness take her.

A gasp rose from the crowd. Just as she was about to pitch forward into the grave, someone grabbed her and pulled her back, with a hand that seemed capable and comforting, yet cold and dangerous. A hand that was scarred and battered, yet beautiful and strong. Erin opened her eyes and felt Detective Slade's grip tighten on her arm.

"Are you all right?"

"I...felt faint," she said weakly. His hand was still on her arm, and beneath the fabric of her coat, Erin imagined that she could feel the warmth of his hand seeping through her. Her skin tingled with awareness, with warning. Her heart began to thud against her chest as he guided her away from the grave.

He'd turned up the collar on his black leather coat,

but he didn't have an umbrella, and his dark hair glistened with droplets of water. She'd forgotten how tall he was, how formidable he appeared. He was still wearing the dark glasses she found so daunting, but even guarded, his stare was powerful, mesmerizing, as he gazed down at her. Suddenly Erin remembered last night and how his gaze had seemed to trap her.

"Rough day" was all he said, guiding her out of the cemetery toward the street. But somehow those two simple words conveyed everything Erin was experiencing at that moment. She wanted to cry and gave silent thanks for the mask of rain on her face.

At the edge of the graveyard, she stopped and looked back. The tombstones blurred in the rain, creating an eerie, almost mystical illusion. Someone was watching her, she thought. Someone was watching her *again*, and she shuddered, a dark portent creeping over her. She looked up and found Detective Slade gazing down at her with hidden eyes.

"What is it?" His voice held an edge, as if he knew—or sensed—what she was feeling.

But Erin didn't want to admit even to herself that she was suddenly, desperately afraid. She hugged her arms to her chest, then shrugged. What could she say? That her imagination was running away with her? That she was seeing monsters now, even in daylight?

As if sensing her reluctance, Slade let the matter drop. Without another word, they began walking again. After a few moments, Erin said, "How is the investigation progressing?"

It was his turn to shrug. "As well as can be expected."

"What did the autopsy report show?"

Slade hesitated. "We can talk about that later."

"I want to hear it now," Erin said, mustering her courage. She braced her shoulders as if to prove to Slade she could handle whatever he had to say. "What was the exact cause of Megan's death, Detective? I want to know."

Again that odd hesitation. "There were marks on her neck."

"Marks? You mean she was strangled?" That would explain why there was no blood that night, Erin thought.

Detective Slade stared straight ahead as they continued to walk. "Your sister wasn't strangled," he said.

"But I thought you said—"

"There were marks on her neck. Two puncture wounds. Almost all of Megan's blood was drained from her body."

Erin staggered to a stop. A wave of horror washed over her. Slade's hand shot out and steadied her once more, but Erin was hardly aware of it. Instead, in her mind she saw an image of Megan's body on the ground, the smile on her lips. Erin put a hand to her mouth as her stomach churned sickeningly. "My

God," she said. "What kind of person could do that? Especially to Megan. She was so young, so beautiful...." And now she was dead. Dear God, Erin wrote about this kind of stuff. It didn't happen in real life. Not to Megan. Please not to Megan.

"How did he do it?' she asked weakly.

"We don't know for sure."

"*Why* did he do it? What kind of monster would do such a thing?"

Slade said nothing, but Erin barely noticed. Her mind was racing with the implications. "What if it was because of me?" she whispered. "What if this happened because of my book?"

Slade was still holding her arm, and now his grip tightened. "You had nothing to do with this."

Erin lifted her agonized gaze. "How can you be so sure? There are a lot of people out there who read my books. What if one of them decided to..."

"There are a lot of people out there," Slade said evenly, "who have never read your books. And they kill, anyway."

"But do they drain their victim's blood?" Erin's heart was beating so fast she felt light-headed. She swayed again, and Slade steadied her once more.

His mouth tightened as he gazed down at her. "We'll get him, Erin. I promise you that. He won't get away with this."

"No, he won't," she agreed, the horror inside her

turning to rage. "He won't get away with this. I'll see to that."

"What do you mean?"

They stared at each other in silence. Mist shrouded them in an illusion of privacy, and once again Erin became conscious of how tall he was, how immense he looked in that long black coat. She hadn't been aware of how far their walk had taken them, but as she looked around now, she realized the cemetery was long behind them. They stood in the gray afternoon, a myriad of desolate buildings surrounding them, and all Erin could think was how quiet everything seemed. How alone they were.

Behind his dark glasses, Slade continued to hold her gaze. Erin's fingers began to tremble, so she forced her hands deep into the pockets of her coat.

"What did you mean you'll see to it?" he repeated suspiciously. His voice was low and rough. She could see the hint of anger in the rigid set of his mouth, a mouth she knew could look at once cruel and sensuous....

Erin tilted her chin, denying her thoughts. "I mean I can help you find him. I knew my sister better than anyone else. If anyone can trace the last few days of her life, it would be me."

"Don't be stupid."

He drew her up so close the frost of their breath mingled in the cold air. Their bodies were almost, but not quite, touching, yet Erin had no difficulty at all imagining the warmth of his skin next to hers. The hardness of his body against hers...

Dear God, she thought. What am I doing? What am I thinking?

Megan was gone, dead and buried. She was never coming back. How could Erin be having these feelings for a man she knew absolutely nothing about? A man who seemed to embody her deepest fears?

Guilt, as sharp as a dagger, stabbed through her.

"Think about it," she insisted, willing the beat of her heart to slow. She tried to swallow away the sudden dryness in her throat. "Her friends would be more likely to talk to me than they would to the police. There's no telling what I might learn. At any rate, I *want* to talk to them. I want to find out everything I can about my sister. I have to," she finished, her voice giving away the desperation she felt. "I have to know why she died the way she did."

"Listen to me," he said, his voice deep and dark and full of warning. "You have no idea what we're dealing with here. You have no idea how much danger you could be in if you start talking to the wrong people, going to the wrong places. Stay out of it, Erin. Let me do my job."

"How can I be sure you'll do your job?" Erin challenged, feeling her anger flare. His fingers warmed her arm through the fabric of her coat, made her skin burn with awareness, but she wouldn't pull away. She wouldn't give him the satisfaction of knowing how deeply his touch affected her.

Slade smiled a thin, humorless smile. "So that's it. You think you can do a better job than the police. You think you can find clues we wouldn't uncover. You think you can play amateur detective and not get burned. *Think again, Erin.* Think long and hard before you do something you and I both might regret."

His hand fell away from her arm, but Erin's skin still flamed from his touch. He gazed down at her for a moment longer, then he turned and headed back toward the cemetery, his long coat flapping in the wind.

Erin took a deep breath, trying to quell the rapid throb of the pulse in her throat. She watched him disappear into the mist. The dark glasses, the scars, the grim facade. She wished she could see him just once, on her own terms, in broad daylight, with the sun pouring down on them and the shadows and mist that seemed to envelop him nothing more than a memory.

He's a policeman, she reminded herself. A cop. That alone explained her wariness. Erin could still remember clearly the detective who had investigated her mother's disappearance. Cold, impersonal, with a rumpled demeanor and a bad disposition, he had looked at Erin and Megan as distastefully as if they'd been something he'd scraped off his shoe.

Within days he'd stopped taking their aunt's calls.

He'd never called them back, never come by the apartment to give them any news. Erin remembered how helpless she'd felt, how at the mercy of that indifferent detective she'd been. What could an eight-year-old kid do about it, though?

But Erin was no longer a child. She was twenty-six years old, and she knew better than to depend on anyone but herself for the answers she needed. What if her book *had* caused Megan's death? What if some psycho had believed himself to be her demon lover? How could Erin live with the guilt, with not knowing for sure?

No matter what Detective Slade said, Erin knew she couldn't rest until Megan's murderer had been brought to justice. It was the last thing, the *only* thing she could do for her sister. And for herself.

Squaring her shoulders, Erin turned and started walking. She knew the limo that had driven her from the church still waited for her at the cemetery, but she couldn't go back there now. She didn't want to face Detective Slade, but more than that, she didn't want to have to say goodbye to Megan again. Not after what she'd learned.

Someone called to Slade as he unlocked his car at the curb, and he paused, glancing over his shoulder. Dr. Traymore walked toward him, his face shielded by the brim of the felt hat he was wearing.

"A lovely ceremony," he commented, nodding his head toward the cemetery.

"If you like funerals," Slade said.

"At my age they can be a very moving experience," Traymore remarked. "However, this one was particularly disturbing to me. I hope the necessary precautions were taken with the body, Detective. The burial was quite hasty."

"Do you want a blow-by-blow account of the autopsy?" Slade returned angrily, remembering Erin's questions. Had he told her too much? He was walking a fine line, he knew. He'd hoped that by revealing the nature of Megan's death to Erin, it might frighten her into taking the first plane back to L.A., before it was too late. Unfortunately, he'd seen no indication of that from her earlier.

Damn, now the old man was beginning to worry him, too. Slade suspected Traymore knew just enough to be dangerous. If he started poking his nose in the wrong places, started asking more questions...

Dr. Traymore's eyes grew even more grim as his gaze drifted back to the cemetery. "I pray you did the right thing, Detective," he said slowly. "I pray you are who and what I think you are. Because if you're not, there's a very good chance that at midnight tonight Megan Ramsey will rise from her grave, starving for blood."

Erin walked for hours in the rain and mist until finally exhaustion drove her toward home. A lighted window in a bookstore on the corner near the apartment caught her eye, and she stopped for a moment, staring at a display featuring her books. Almost ten years' worth of work. A decade of her life dedicated to exorcising the demons from her past, and what had it gotten her?

Not much, she reflected. Money, success, a small measure of satisfaction, to be sure. But she was still alone, still haunted by memories. The one serious relationship she'd ever had had begun for all the wrong reasons and had ended badly. Never again would she put herself in the position of needing someone, of depending on anyone other than herself. Never again would she freely give her trust.

After all, Erin thought, grimacing, if you couldn't trust your own mother, who could you trust?

She glanced back at her books in the window. The cover of *Demon Lover* leapt out at her. The picture of the vampire seemed just a little too realistic tonight, perhaps because of what she'd learned about Megan's death. The long white fangs gleamed in the subdued light from the window, and his eyes—dark, mesmerizing, soul-stealing eyes—held her in thrall. And for some reason, Erin thought of the dark figure she'd seen at the cemetery.

Had he been real?

Or had the same imagination that had created the vampire she was looking at now conjured up the dark, menacing figure that had beckoned to her, that had whispered to her soul?

What kind of mind would give birth to such a creature? she thought in disgust. What kind of person would be obsessed by such darkness? What kind of woman would be drawn to the thing that frightened her the most?

Erin tried to shake off the gloom her thoughts brought on, but the wind blowing through the trees carried a faint whisper to her ears, making her wonder again if she could truly distinguish between fantasy and reality.

*Erin. We've been waiting for you, Erin.*

Water puddled on the streets and reflected long, wavering beams of light against the pavement. Dead leaves rattled along the sidewalk in front of her, and as Erin hurried toward the apartment, she pulled her coat more tightly around her, trying to protect herself from the coming night.

But the darkness seeped through the woolen fabric. It oozed through her skin and slivered into her soul. It made her wonder if she would ever be warm again.

The hair at the back of her neck prickled as she glanced over her shoulder. How deserted the streets seemed suddenly. It was barely twilight, but the rain made it seem much later. Gloom hung over the city like a London fog. Erin could feel its oppressive weight bearing down on her shoulders as if invisible hands were holding her back. She hurried her steps, but the apartment seemed to get farther and farther away.

Someone was watching her. She couldn't shake the feeling. Someone was watching her from the darkness, waiting for the chance to—

A dark figure stepped from a doorway and blocked her path. Erin gasped, tried to move around him, but he moved with her. Don't panic, she cautioned herself. Don't make any sudden moves.

She'd lived in the city all her life. It wasn't the first time she'd been accosted on the street, but there was something particularly frightening about the way this man stood in front of her, smiling down at her as if he knew her deepest, darkest secrets. And for one impossible, irrational moment, she thought the cover of *Demon Lover* had come to life before her very eyes.

*We've been waiting for you, Erin.*

He hadn't spoken aloud, but Erin could have sworn she heard his exact thoughts. He was tall, impossibly thin, with long black hair pulled back into a ponytail. His skin was dark and swarthy, with the look of the Mediterranean, and his eyes were jet black.

As her heart pounded inside her chest, Erin thought briefly that he was the most handsome man she'd ever seen. It wasn't...human to be so perfect, and suddenly an image of Detective Slade's scarred hands swept into her mind.

The man in front of her frowned. He made a low

growling sound in his throat that sent shivers of dread racing up and down Erin's spine. He no longer looked handsome or perfect or even like a man, for that matter. He looked cold. Evil. Bestial. *Like a vampire.* Erin reached for her cross, then discovered it was no longer there.

The black gaze followed her hand to her throat as if anticipating the emptiness she would find there. Then slowly his eyes moved back up to her face, lingering on her lips. He smiled, his white teeth gleaming in the reflected light. No fangs, she noticed in fleeting relief, but in the next moment, Erin thought of the man at the cemetery. The menacing figure that had beckoned her to follow him into darkness. The man who would have seen her drop the silver cross into Megan's grave.

"Who are you?" she whispered.

"Don't you know?" he said.

"What do you want?" she demanded.

"Don't you know?"

His voice seemed to echo from a deep, dark well. His smile deepened when he saw her shiver. His eyes taunted her as he reached out and caressed her barren neck with one fingertip, tracing the invisible line of the cross. Erin shrank from his icy touch. Her stomach recoiled from the feel of his flesh against hers, and she thought her heart would thrash its way out of her chest.

She took a faltering step back from him. When he

made no move toward her, she kept backing away until she felt the curb against her feet. Then she turned and dashed into the street.

A car screamed to a halt just inches from hitting her, and a horn blasted in her ears, but Erin didn't stop. She raced across the street and only then, safely on the other side, did she dare to look back.

The man was gone, dissolved like smoke into the night. Had *he* been real?

She could still feel his icy finger on her skin. He'd been real, all right. The streets of New York were filled with crazies like him. He'd wanted nothing more than to frighten her. Erin supposed she should feel lucky. At least she still had her purse. And her life.

Another breeze gusted through the trees overhead, and for a moment, she thought she heard the sound of male laughter in the wind. She ran through the twilight, her heels clicking against the pavement.

Erin took the steps of the apartment building two at a time, dragged open the door and fled inside. At the top of the stairs, her numb fingers fumbled with the key to Megan's apartment. With a muttered, "Damn," she tugged off her glove with her teeth and tried the key again. Downstairs, she heard the front door open and close softly, then someone stepped into the corridor.

Erin's heart jumped into her throat. Dear God, he had followed her home. Frantically she jiggled the key in the lock. "Come on," she urged, casting a terrified glance over her shoulder. She could hear his footsteps on the stairs now, heard the telltale squeak as he reached the middle of the steps. Then the steps moved upward, toward the landing, where Erin stood trapped.

Her hands were shaking so badly she dropped the key. She heard it thump against the worn carpet, but in the murky light, she couldn't see it. With a gasping oath, she dropped to her knees and ran her palms along the dirty floor until she felt the cool metal against her flesh. She jumped up and jammed the key into the lock so brutally she thought for a moment she might have bent it.

Then the key turned smoothly, and she could have wept with relief. But just as she pushed the door open, a cold hand closed over hers.

# CHAPTER FOUR

A scream rose in Erin's throat, but before panic had time to set in, she whirled, swinging her purse with all her might at the man's head. The weighted leather connected with his right temple, and he swore viciously. Erin tried to strike again, but this time he was ready for her. His hand reached out and snared her wrist. She cried out as the purse—her only weapon—went flying from her hand.

"Damn it, stop struggling before I have to hurt you," he ordered. It took a second for Erin to realize that the voice wasn't the one she'd just heard on the street, but one that was more familiar. Maybe even more frightening. She shivered as she gazed up at Detective Slade's stoic demeanor. "If I'd been the murderer," he said, "you'd be dead by now."

"Oh, yeah?" she said, rising to his bait, the adrenaline still kicking through her veins. "Then how come you're the one who's bleeding?"

His hand went to his temple. He touched the spot gingerly, then lowered his hand and gazed at the red smear on his fingertips. "Damn," he muttered.

"I'm sorry I hurt you," Erin said. "But you shouldn't have sneaked up on me like that. I thought you were...someone else."

One brow rose over the dark glasses. "Like who?"

"Like the creep I just saw on the street," she said uncomfortably. "I thought he might be trying to mug me or..."

"Or worse?" he supplied coldly. "Where was this man?"

"At the corner, near the bookstore. I think he just wanted to scare me," Erin said hastily, trying to take the edge off her fear. "He didn't hurt me or anything." But she shivered anyway, remembering the man's frozen touch. She hugged her arms to herself as she gazed at Slade. "What are you doing here?"

"I've been trying to call you," Slade said. "I was worried when you didn't come back to the cemetery. Where've you been?"

"Walking."

"All this time?"

His liquid voice flowed over her, cold and dark and oddly coercive.

"I didn't feel like coming back here after the funeral," she said defensively. In fact, she might have been glad to see him if he didn't seem so unapproachable, so formidable. "You needn't have been worried about me. I can take care of myself," she assured him.

"Can you?"

There was something in his tone—a faint challenge?—that made Erin grow even more uneasy. She glanced around the darkened hallway. There was no

one about. No one had even come out to investigate
the commotion. She was completely alone with a man
that made her tremble, with a man that made her think
of moonlight and madness. Of secrets and whispers
and promises that could only be told in the dead of
night.

She looked at him, telling herself she couldn't be
feeling this pull, this strange attraction, for a man who
seemed to embody her deepest fears...and her darkest
nightmares. *What kind of woman would be drawn to
the thing that frightened her the most?*

"He could come after you, you know."

Her gaze shot back to his. For a moment she'd
thought he was talking about the man on the street,
then she said, "You mean the murderer? Why would
he come after me?"

Slade took a step toward her. "You said you saw
something that night."

His face looked even grimmer in the dim hallway
light. His eyes, as always, were hidden, masking
whatever emotions he might have been feeling. Erin
moistened her lips. He looked so tall tonight, so impossibly remote. The darker the night became, the
more imposing he grew. "I didn't see anything," she
protested. "Not really."

"The murderer might not know that. Supposing *he*
saw *you?*"

"You're just trying to frighten me," she said with
false bravado. "I don't even know what I saw. Those

glowing eyes…it was probably just an animal…a cat or something. He won't come after me. It would be too risky.''

''You're assuming that he's rational,'' Slade said. ''You're assuming that he's more than a cold-blooded, vicious animal whose every instinct is to kill. Don't underestimate him, or the danger. That could be a fatal mistake.''

''I won't,'' Erin said angrily, goaded by his tone and by her own fear. ''But don't underestimate me, either. I don't have a death wish, Detective, but neither am I going to cower inside that apartment until he's apprehended. I won't let them scare me away this time.''

''Them?''

''Him. I mean him,'' she said, turning to go inside. Slade's hand reached out and stopped her. A tiny thrill raced up her backbone as his hand closed over hers.

''Let me go first,'' he said, stepping past her and entering the apartment.

Erin retrieved her purse, then followed him inside, watching as he strode across the living room and tested the knob on the French door. She was amazed as always how he seemed to dominate the immediate area.

Maybe it was because he was so tall, well over six foot, with the kind of hard, muscular body that seemed to exude power and strength. Or maybe it was the long, black leather coat he always wore. Or the dark glasses. Or...was it something else about him that intrigued her?

*What kind of woman would be drawn to the thing that frightened her the most?*

"Well?"

His deep voice startled her. Erin's hand fluttered to her throat, but once again she found only the empty space where the cross had once hung. "What?"

"I asked if you'd gotten this lock fixed?"

"No, not yet. The super was supposed to come by yesterday, but he never showed up."

"Does he live here in the building?"

"Yes. He has an apartment on the ground floor."

"I'll speak to him on my way out." Slade walked away from the window and browsed through the photos displayed on the mantel. Then he turned toward her, and Erin's heart flip-flopped inside her chest. He was staring at her neck, much as the man on the street had earlier, and Erin shivered. Slade took another step toward her, and she had to fight the overwhelming urge to retreat. "Why did you put your cross in your sister's grave?" His voice was low and chilling. Deeply compelling.

Erin swallowed, her throat suddenly dry. "I wanted her to be protected."

"From what?"

"From the darkness," she whispered.

"You should have kept it," he said. "You should have kept it for yourself."

"Why? Vampires don't really exist," she said.

"But evil does," he said. "And the danger out there is very real."

Their gazes locked for the longest moment. Erin couldn't see his eyes, but knew without a doubt that his gaze had dropped again to her bare neck. Never had she felt so helpless, so unprotected as she did at that moment.

"I have to go," he said almost reluctantly. "My shift starts soon." He took a card from the inside pocket of his coat and handed it to her. "If you hear any disturbances, see anything suspicious, call me. Don't take any foolish chances. I don't care if you even hear a mouse in the kitchen, you call me. If I'm not in, ask for Detective Christopher. You understand me?"

Erin plucked the card from his fingers. "I understand. Perfectly." She glanced at the card. Nick. His first name was Nick.

He opened the front door, then paused on the threshold to turn back and repeat the warning he'd issued the first night she'd met him, the night Megan had died. "Keep all your doors and windows locked. Don't go out after dark. And whatever you do, don't invite anyone inside." His voice was even, but the emphasis was unmistakable. "Talk to them through the door, on the phone, whatever, *but don't ever invite anyone in here.*"

Then he was gone. And the apartment seemed cold and empty. Menacing.

Erin stared at the closed door for several minutes. His warning echoed in the stillness. *Don't invite anyone inside.* Vampires couldn't enter your home without an invitation. She'd learned that rule years and years ago, and it had given her a small amount of comfort during those dark, sleepless nights when her nightmares had seemed more real than reality. Just don't invite them inside, she'd tell herself.

But now a chilling thought seeped into her mind. Vampires did not exist. And yet... She had already invited two people inside the apartment. Racine DiMeneci and Detective Slade. But surely that legendary rule only applied to strangers. Surely it didn't mean people she knew.

But then, how much did she actually know about Racine? How much did she know about Detective Slade...Nick?

Erin's fingers trembled as she shot home the bolt on the front door because the answer to both questions was exactly the same.

She didn't know anything about either of them.

Slade sat at a table in Nosferatu's, the nightclub Racine DiMeneci had told him and Erin about yesterday. Nosferatu's was also the club where he had first seen Megan Ramsey a few weeks ago.

He gazed around the darkened club as the decadent music swirled around him. Everyone inside the place wore dark glasses and, ironically, Slade's own need to hide his eyes made him blend in even more effectively, made it difficult to distinguish between him and those he hunted.

Actually, he had also seen Racine here with Megan one night and he wondered now when the redhead would make the connection. Things could start getting sticky for him if too many people began asking too many questions. Racine and Dr. Traymore would both eventually have to be dealt with, but Erin Ramsey was his first concern. He had to keep the truth from her at all costs, but already he knew she had suspicions. She couldn't write the stories she wrote without at least halfway believing.

He thought about her assertion that she wanted to help in the investigation, and his mouth thinned. It was his job to make sure she stayed safe, but that meant he'd have to see her again. And if he saw her again, he knew he'd want to touch her, to test for himself the softness of her skin, the silkiness of her hair. And if he touched her once...

Don't, he warned himself. Don't think about her that way.

She was exactly the kind of woman who could prove dangerous to a man like him. The kind of woman who could look into his eyes and gaze deeply into his soul. The kind of woman who could learn all his secrets, no matter how hard he tried to guard himself against her.

There had been another woman like that once... another woman a lifetime ago....

A vision materialized in his mind, and for a moment, Slade allowed himself to remember Simone's face. But he didn't remember the innocence. Nor the youth and the beauty and the trust that had once radiated from her visage when she'd looked at him. What he saw—what he made himself see—was the evil she had become.

Because of him.

Slade's fists clenched tightly as he tried to shut off the memories, but they were coming back stronger than ever tonight. Erin Ramsey had done that to him. She had made him remember who and what he was. She had reminded him of what could never be again.

He ripped off his dark glasses and passed a weary hand over his eyes. But almost immediately he replaced the glasses. He didn't want people looking into his eyes. Didn't want people staring into his soul. Didn't want people reading the truth about him.

The music swirled around him, sensuous and seductive, and he watched the bodies writhing on the dance floor. How many of them would leave here, their souls untouched? How many of them were even now fighting the blood lust that tormented their every waking moment, from sundown to sunup? What truths would be revealed if everyone removed their dark glasses?

He sighed deeply, feeling the gloom of the place settle over him. He always felt depressed, coming here, and yet he couldn't stay away. Couldn't keep from warning the innocent young women who strayed in here, looking for thrills. Couldn't help trying to protect others as he hadn't been able to protect Simone.

Eight years ago, he thought, staring down at his scarred hands. Eight years ago he'd come here with Simone, the night they'd gotten engaged. She'd been so young then. So beautiful and innocent.

Or so he'd thought.

But Simone had been taken with Nosferatu's the moment they'd stepped inside. The dark, eerie atmosphere. The loud, erotic music. The curtained alcoves that hid only God knew what. She'd been drawn to it all in a way Slade hadn't understood. Then.

They'd met Drake D'Angelo here that night. He'd appeared out of nowhere, a tall, gaunt stranger who had captivated Simone the moment he'd touched her hand.

Slade squeezed his eyes closed, trying to stem the memories, but try as he might, he couldn't keep them away. He knew that. Every time he set foot in this place, it was his way of making restitution for Simone's life. For her soul.

That night, after they'd gotten home, Slade remembered how wildly passionate Simone had been. How…untamed her lovemaking had been. He'd never seen her like that, and the next day he'd started to wonder why. Had she been thinking about him when they were making love, or had she been thinking of D'Angelo? Had she been dreaming about that dark stranger? Wanting him as Slade had held her in his arms?

And then, a few days after they'd met D'Angelo, Slade's worst fears came true. Simone told him she was in love with someone else.

For days after she'd left him, the pain and jealousy festered inside Slade until he could stand it no longer. He knew he had to see Simone again, appeal to her one last time before he could turn loose the past.

He got the address from the police department files, then drove to D'Angelo's house on Riverside Drive. The mansion was dark and the air around it damp and rife with decay. The door was open, as if D'Angelo had somehow known he was coming. Letting his eyes adjust to the gloom, Slade walked cautiously down first one corridor, then the next.

In a candlelit room that overlooked the river, he found the lovers together. Simone wore a filmy red dress that hid nothing of her lush figure, and her long dark hair cascaded down her back in thick, wanton curls. If anything, she looked even more beautiful than Slade remembered as she lay with her head tilted back, her slim white neck exposed to D'Angelo's kisses.

"Simone!"

She gasped and whirled, her hand automatically going to her mouth. Something red was smeared across her lips and two trickles of blood coursed down her neck. Slowly she stood and faced Slade. The gossamer gown she wore billowed around her legs and plunged low at her breasts. She looked beautiful, seductive, feral.

And evil.

There was a strange glow in her eyes, an eerie half smile on her red-stained lips. As Slade watched, she lifted a fingertip to her neck, wiped away the blood, then raised the finger to her lips. Slade's stomach rolled sickeningly.

Simone smiled. "Nicholas. How sweet of you to visit us," she purred, and D'Angelo, reclining on the bed, laughed, a deep, dark, mirthless sound that chilled Slade to the bone.

"Yes, come in, by all means. Simone, aren't you going to welcome your old friend with a kiss?"

Simone was still smiling at Slade in a way that made him shudder. Slowly she walked across the room toward him, the sheer fabric of her gown rippling in the breeze from the open terrace doorway. She lifted a hand and touched his face. Slade had to fight the urge to flinch from her. Her touch was cold, lifeless. No longer human.

"Simone," he whispered, forcing his hand to close around hers, "what has he done to you?"

"Kiss me," she pleaded. Slade fought to keep the contents of his stomach from rebelling. Something was not right here. Almost against his will, he took a step back, away from her.

Simone pursed her red lips, pouting. "Oh, Nick, don't. Don't run away from me. Remember the way it used to be? The way you used to kiss me? It was so good. Do it again. Do it now. Kiss me, Nick. Just one last kiss…"

Dear God, how he wanted to! Even as repulsed as he was by her, a part of him still yearned to take her in his arms, to pretend the last few days had only been a nightmare. Simone belonged to him. She was his first love, his only love. They could still be together, still have the life they had planned for so long. Without her, his life was meaningless, a wasteland.

"We can still be together," she whispered as if reading his mind.

"Simone." He murmured her name, brushed her cold, flawless cheek with his knuckles. "I still love you. I still want you."

"Then kiss me, my love."

How could he resist? He loved her so much. Wanted her so much. Slade bent toward her. Her eyes drifted closed as she waited for him, waited for his kiss. A tear coursed down her cheek, and Slade realized that it had fallen from his own eyes. "Simone," he whispered. "Dear God…"

Over Simone's shoulder, Slade saw D'Angelo move in the shadows. His eyes gleamed like silver moondrops in the darkness, and for the first time since he'd entered D'Angelo's house, Slade felt afraid. Terrified. Not for himself, but for Simone.

"What have you done to her?" he demanded.

"You pathetic human," D'Angelo growled. "I did nothing to Simone that she didn't want. She and I are meant to be together. I've waited centuries for someone like her. She loves the darkness. Craves it. There's nothing you can do to keep us apart."

"We'll see about that," Slade shouted. He grabbed Simone's hand. "We're getting out of here. Now! You don't know what he is, what he can do to you." Neither did Slade. But he knew without a doubt that D'Angelo was evil, and he had to get Simone away from him.

Simone lifted her dazed eyes to his. "Oh, but I do. I know exactly who and what he is. He's given me eternal life, and I can give it to you. I can make you one of us." She opened her mouth and laughed, revealing long fangs that gleamed in the candlelight.

"Dear God," Slade gasped in horror.

Simone reached for him, her teeth growing even longer, sharper, more deadly as she lifted her mouth to his neck. Terrified, Slade tried to shove her back, but she was too strong. Her arms closed around him, holding him to her even as he felt those deadly fangs graze his flesh.

He experienced little more than two pinpricks of pain, but he felt the darkness almost immediately seeping into his soul. Felt the coldness of her touch draining away his warmth, and for a moment, dear God, for one split second, he welcomed it. Desired it. *Craved* it.

Then somehow he managed to summon the courage to fling her away from him. To tear himself away from that sinister pleasure that beckoned so strongly. Simone's arms flailed wide, upsetting one of the silver candelabras on the table near the window.

Instantly the drapery caught fire, and the breeze fanned the flames. The blaze raced across the carpet. Within seconds, an inferno separated Slade and Simone from D'Angelo. The vampire roared in rage. "Simone!"

Simone turned on Slade. "You fool! Look what you made me do!"

Slade grabbed her arm. "Leave him," he pleaded. "Come with me, Simone. We'll find someone who can help us. It's not too late. It can't be too late."

"Don't you understand?" she screamed. "It's too late for both of us now!" Her fangs had disappeared and she looked lovely and innocent, exactly like the Simone he had fallen in love with years ago. "I belong to him now."

Before Slade could stop her, Simone had turned

and plunged into the wall of fire. Slade ran after her, tried to reach her, tried to draw her back. The pain in his seared hands was nothing compared to the torment in his heart. Before his very eyes, he saw Simone's gossamer gown erupt in flames, but somehow she continued through the blaze, trying in vain to reach D'Angelo's outstretched arms.

"Slade!" D'Angelo screamed, his own flesh blazing as he clutched Simone in his arms. "I'll see you in hell, Slade!"

Whether from the burns on his hands or from Simone's last deadly kiss, Slade never knew, but he blacked out then. When he came to, he found himself outside on the grass as the mansion blazed like a gigantic torch in the night. Lying there watching the fire, Slade felt his world turn to ashes around him.

When it was all over, nothing remained but Slade's guilt and the endless questions he'd had to face from the department. What was he doing at D'Angelo's mansion? How did he know the man? Did he go there with the intent to harm him?

The questions very nearly ended Slade's career with the force because he couldn't answer them. How could he? How could he make people believe what he still couldn't understand himself? If not for Simone's father, the police commissioner, Slade's career would have been finished.

But the commissioner had witnessed the changes in his daughter. Convinced that what Slade had told him was true, Thomas Delaney then formed a very special, very elite, very secret organization within the police department. And Slade had been his first recruit.

But Slade's devotion to the Mission, his own personal crusade to wipe out the vampire population in New York City had not been without a price. What he saw when he looked in the mirror now was a creature almost as soulless as the monsters he stalked at night. What he saw was a man who belonged neither to the light nor to the dark, but one who skirted the very brink of each. He saw a man who had been branded by the evil of Simone's kiss, his eyes now too sensitive to light. A man who was forced to live his life almost exclusively in the night.

Just like the creatures he sought to obliterate.

What if someone had seen him with Megan Ramsey that night? All those old questions would surface again, and that whole mess from his past would be dredged up. The Mission could be threatened. The one thing that gave Slade's life any meaning at all could be destroyed. And without that, there was nothing to set him apart from the other creatures who hunted the night.

"Nick?" Fighting the memories and the terrible guilt descending over him, Slade looked up. A young woman stood at his table, gazing down at him from behind her own dark glasses. "May I sit down?"

"What are you doing here, Christina?" Slade

asked harshly as she slipped into a chair, facing him. "How many times have I told you to stay away from this place?"

"I know," Christina said. "I know you promised to help me, but I had to come here tonight. I had to see you." She pulled off her dark glasses, and Slade noticed with relief that her eyes were still very clear and very blue. Not silver. Not glowing. Her blond hair gleamed with life as she leaned across the table toward him, and when she tentatively smiled, deep dimples graced the corners of her mouth. She was barely eighteen, and her appearance remained childlike and innocent. Christina Harris seemed the epitome of the girl next door. Except for the fact that, for some unknown reason, she was increasingly drawn to the darkness.

"I gave you my number," Slade said angrily. "We could have met somewhere else."

"I didn't want to take the chance of anyone else finding out I'd contacted you," she said secretively. "I knew you'd come back here sooner or later." Her anxious gaze scanned the club for a moment, then came back to rest on Slade. She leaned even closer toward him. "I think I know who killed Megan Ramsey," she said.

Slade's hand shot out and ensnared her slender wrist. "Who? Damn it, tell me what you know."

Again Christina's gaze raked the club, a little more

frantically this time. "I can't," she said. "Not here. It's too dangerous. Meet me."

"Where?"

"Tomorrow night. In the alley outside. I'll be there after midnight."

"No," Slade said. "I don't want you anywhere near this place. We'll leave here together. Now."

"No! We have to do it my way. You'll know why tomorrow night. You can trust me, Nick. I owe you my life. I'll never forget that night... What would have happened to me if you hadn't come along...?" Her words trailed away as she lowered her eyes.

Images of that night flashed through Slade's mind. The vampire had lured Christina outside the club and had been ready to sink his fangs into her neck when Slade found them. If Slade hadn't destroyed the vampire, Christina would be dead now. Or worse.

Christina's gaze lifted. "You helped me, Nick. Now I want to help you."

"Why can't you tell me tonight?" Slade demanded suspiciously. "I don't like this, Christina."

"I know," she said worriedly, "but I'm taking too much of a risk as it is just talking to you, being seen with you. Please," she begged, "don't follow me out of here. I don't want to end up like Megan."

Slade watched her go. Her last plea effectively doused any idea he might have had of following her, of demanding she tell him here and now what she knew.

*I don't want to end up like Megan.* What the hell had she meant by that? Why had talking to him scared her so badly?

Slade scanned the bodies on the dance floor, the looming shadows in the alcoves. Was he here? Was the vampire who had killed Megan Ramsey watching and waiting in the darkness? Had he seen Slade talking to Christina?

Slade glanced at his watch. It was getting late, and as much as he wanted to find Christina again, to see her safely out of this place, he knew he couldn't. He had to be somewhere. He had to make sure someone else was safe tonight.

He tried to tamp down the feeling of urgency rushing through him, but he found himself thinking of Erin Ramsey again. He imagined her alone in that apartment, frightened, unprotected. He thought about her warm skin and her scented hair....

His heart started pounding and his pulse raced. It was almost midnight, and he was here and she was there. An unprecedented sense of danger surged through him as he strode from the club into the night.

It was almost midnight. The clock on the mantel ticked off the minutes as the shadows outside grew deeper, the night darker.

*"Do you believe in vampires?"*

Try as she might, Erin couldn't seem to get Megan's last question out of her mind. She went over and over their final conversation, remembering the quiet excitement in Megan's voice when she'd urged Erin to come back to New York to see the play that Megan was starring in.

"It has a vampire hero, just like in your *Demon Lover*. Don't you love the coincidence?" Megan had said, and then laughed.

But it hadn't been the coincidence or the excitement in her sister's voice that had brought Erin back here. What had brought her back, she realized now, was the question her sister had asked her at the onset of their conversation.

*"Do you believe in vampires?"*

Erin closed her eyes, thinking about her latest book, the novel which she had thought at the time had precipitated Megan's question. Now, as she sat in Megan's apartment going through her sister's things, Erin had to wonder if Megan's question—her fascination with the supernatural as Racine had suggested—had been prompted by something else. Something more than their bleak past. Something more than a book or a play. Something more... terrifyingly real.

*"Do you believe in vampires?"*

*What kind of woman would be drawn to the thing that frightened her the most?*

Was that the real reason she'd come back? Erin asked herself. To confront the monsters of her past?

To prove to herself once and for all that she *didn't* believe?

Had Megan believed? Had she succumbed to the darkness both of them had been terrified of years ago? Had she come to...welcome it, instead?

The deeper Erin dug into Megan's personal belongings, the more intrigued she became with her sister's life, and the more convinced she became that, as close as she and Megan had once been, in many ways—in important ways—Erin hadn't really known her sister at all. Not at the end.

She only had to look in Megan's closet to realize that fact. Where once they had both dressed in pastel colors and simple styles, now Megan's wardrobe consisted of dozens of sexy outfits, mainly in black. Obviously Megan's tastes had changed dramatically. Had she started dressing for a man? Erin wondered. A man who reminded her of Erin's demon lover?

In the distance, Erin heard the chimes as the clock in the living room struck midnight. A strange chill crept up her spine as she fingered Megan's clothing. Some essence of her sister still seemed to linger in the soft folds of fabric. Erin closed her eyes, concentrating. And as the chimes fell silent, the feeling that she was no longer alone enveloped her.

Terror, as cold and black as an ocean, swept over her.

"Megan?" She whispered the name aloud, sensing a presence.

A breeze, as soft as an illusion, whispered through the room, stirring potpourri in a glass bowl atop Megan's dressing table. The scent of roses filled the room. Bloodred roses. Megan's favorite…

"Megan." The name slipped from Erin's lips with more certainty this time. Her heart pounded in fear as the breeze drifted over her, lifting the loose tendrils of hair, caressing the skin at her nape. Touching her…

*We've been waiting for you, Erin.*

Not Megan's voice, but a man's voice, taunting and elusive.

*Close your eyes. Feel me.*

The breeze brushed her lips, and Erin gasped, terrified by the sudden thrill racing through her.

*Dress for me. Make me desire you.*

Erin tried to deny the voice in her head, tried to fight the compulsive urge to obey it. But she no longer had control of her actions. As if watching herself from a distance, Erin saw herself lifting one of Megan's dresses from its hanger and slipping into it, then turning to face herself in the mirror.

Long and black with a slit up the thigh and cutaway sleeves that bared her shoulders, the dress completely transformed her. Her hair was no longer worn up, but flowed wantonly over her shoulders, down her back. Gone was the woman who harbored her secrets deep within. For just a moment, Erin was no longer Erin. She was a woman who didn't run from the darkness.

A woman who didn't hide from the monsters. She was a woman who embraced the night.

The woman in the mirror was no longer Erin, but Megan.

A man appeared at her side, his reflection obscured so that Erin got merely an impression of his imposing height. He bent and touched his lips to Megan's neck, and Erin felt the sting of his kiss, the deep, dark thrill of his touch. She laughed, a throaty, self-satisfied sound.

Erin took a step closer to the mirror, her hands brushing down her sides, caressing her curves as the man in the mirror caressed her sister's reflection. She knew everything her sister was feeling. She experienced the thrill, the desperate craving.

Suddenly Megan's laugh turned into a scream as the man's kiss deepened. Erin felt a sharp, piercing pain at the side of her neck, and then a wave of darkness began to roll over her. As the lifeblood flowed from her body into his, she experienced a pleasure so intense that she was lifted up and sent soaring.

And then the darkness engulfed her. A blackness so complete Erin knew she could never fight her way out of it overwhelmed her. Dimly she heard another voice calling to her, but she couldn't be sure if it was outside her window or inside her head. It was a male voice that sounded strangely enough like Detective Slade's. Almost instantly, the image in the mirror shattered, but not before Erin saw her sister's discarded body fall to the ground.

Then Erin's own knees buckled, and the floor rushed up to meet her.

# CHAPTER FIVE

Erin opened her eyes and gazed around. Sunlight streamed through the window and slanted across her face. Automatically she threw up a hand to protect herself from the glare. It took her a moment to orient her senses, then she realized she was lying on the floor in her sister's bedroom.

Had she fainted? She frowned, lifting a weak hand to her forehead as she struggled to remember what had happened. She'd been going through Megan's belongings last night and then—

Dear God, she thought, squeezing her eyes tightly shut. She'd read Megan's script, she remembered—a story about a vampire. She must have fallen asleep and had a nightmare. That was the only possible explanation for the vision she'd seen in the mirror and for the feelings she'd experienced that had not been her own, but Megan's.

The man's image in the mirror came back to her, and without thinking Erin touched the side of her neck, remembering the terror, the intense pleasure.

"Vampires don't have reflections," she murmured. It *had* to have been her imagination. "You don't exist," she said more forcefully. "I made you up."

But Megan was dead. Megan was dead because the

blood had been drained from her body by a...a what? A psycho? Or a vampire? Did Erin really believe that? Did she dare?

She squinted again in the sunlight. Megan's bedroom window faced west. It had to be late afternoon, which meant that Erin had slept for more than fifteen hours straight. It was frightening to think of losing so much time. Of being unconscious during the night. Of losing control.

And becoming vulnerable to the monsters that came out while she slept.

She'd even dreamed she heard Detective Slade calling to her. Strange that she should cast him in the role of protector. Even though he was a policeman, when she'd first seen him, Erin remembered thinking how very much he looked like something spawned by her nightmares. A demon lover...

Erin fought for balance as she struggled to her feet, then stood for a moment clutching a post on the canopied bed. Out of the corner of her eye, she caught a glimpse of herself in the mirror. She was still wearing Megan's dress, and her stomach rolled sickeningly.

What's happening to me? she thought desperately. God in heaven, why had she come back here? She should have stayed away. She should never have challenged the monsters, because at that moment, Erin had the terrifying feeling that they were winning. That they were luring her slowly but surely into the darkness.

Just as they had lured Megan.

Trying to fight back her panic, Erin tore off the black dress and tossed it onto the floor of the closet. She grabbed a pair of jeans and a sweater from her suitcase, and headed for the bathroom. For a long time, she stood under the steaming water, trying to make sense of everything that had happened since she'd returned to New York after being away for so long.

New York…the very name conjured up images of darkness and demons. Of monsters waiting all these years for her to come back.

Shivering, Erin turned off the shower and toweled herself dry. ''I've got to get out of here,'' she muttered, trying to avoid her reflection in the bathroom mirror.

Fresh air. That was what she needed. Fresh air, sunshine and miles between herself and this apartment. When she had dressed, Erin grabbed her purse and coat, and hurried out into the late-afternoon sunlight.

Surrounded by vacant warehouses and aging brick buildings converted into vintage clothing shops and alternative music stores, the Alucard Theater was located at the end of an obscure little street in the Village.

Erin stood on the sidewalk, gazing up at the dark facade of the theater. A handbill posted on the locked front door announced the premiere of Roman Gerard's play, *Dark Obsession,* two nights away. It would have been Megan's opening night, Erin thought.

A movement on a tiny balcony overlooking the front of the theater caught her eye and she looked up. She grew uneasy, imagining that someone was standing there watching her. Racine's words about the director came back to haunt her.

"Roman Gerard is practically a recluse," the redhead had told her when Erin had questioned her about the director. "Rumor has it he was in some sort of accident that left him horribly disfigured. No one ever sees him now. He stays in the balcony and issues the stage directions from the shadows."

Images from *Phantom of the Opera* leapt to Erin's mind. She had visions of some poor, hideously deformed creature watching her from above. She'd read enough from Megan's script to know that the brooding protagonist of *Dark Obsession* was a vampire, but unlike the demon lover in Erin's book, a monster who embodied evil, Gerard's vampire was a tortured creature who sought justice in an unjust world. A lonely soul who yearned for the love of a woman who could understand him. Who would embrace the darkness with him. Who would walk through eternity at his side.

Erin's vampire was destroyed in the end.

Gerard's vampire triumphed over those who sought to destroy him.

Erin's gaze lifted again, drawn by another movement on the balcony. The wind stirred a set of wind chimes, and a hanging basket swung to and fro. There's your phantom, she scolded herself. Some detective you'd make.

Still, she couldn't shake the disquieting notion that she was being watched. As the shadows on the street grew even longer, Erin tried to shove away the darkness of her thoughts and concentrate on finding a way into the theater. More than anything, she wanted to talk to Roman Gerard, to find out why he had cast her sister in a play about vampires.

Following the side street that ran parallel to the theater, Erin located the stage door. As she reached for the knob, the wind in the street picked up, rustling leaves in the alley and stirring trash in the gutter. The hair at the back of her neck prickled as her hand slowly turned the knob. The door opened and a man stood staring at her from the darkness within.

"What the hell are you doing here?" he growled.

Erin jumped back and would have stumbled over the concrete step at the stage door if a scarred hand hadn't reached out from the darkness and snagged her wrist. Her throat closed over a scream as she watched Detective Slade step out of the theater into the fading light.

He was wearing his long black coat and the dark

glasses, and for a moment, Erin thought he looked no more substantial than one of the shadows moving in the breeze. But the hand on her wrist, warm, flowing with life, was real enough. Erin's own blood began to pound in her ears.

"What are you doing here?" he repeated.

"I wanted to talk to Roman Gerard."

"About what?"

"About Megan, of course." He was being purposely dense, she thought, just to goad her.

"I thought I told you to leave the investigation to me."

"And I thought I told you that I don't intend to rest until my sister's murderer is caught."

"If you had any sense at all," he said, "you'd be on the first plane out of here."

There was something shocking about his voice. Something raw and elemental about the way he was staring at her. The pulse in Erin's throat began to throb. "Why?" Her voice was hardly more than a whisper. "Do I threaten you that much?"

"You have no idea," he said, his voice rough, angry. He tugged on her wrist, and Erin stumbled toward him. To catch herself, or perhaps to insure some distance between them, Erin put up a hand to his chest. No illusion, this. Beneath her hand was a solid wall, warm and beating with life.

"What are *you* doing here?" she asked.

"Doing my job, believe it or not." His taut voice challenged her to deny it.

They were standing impossibly close, his mouth only a few inches from hers, and something in his expression altered. The challenge melted. The grim line of his mouth softened almost imperceptibly, and his hand moved back to her arm. But not to imprison her this time. To touch her. To hold her. His head moved slightly toward hers.

He was going to kiss her, Erin realized, her heart beating like a drum. He was going to kiss her and she was going to let him. Emotion, stark and wild, swamped her. Not anger any longer. Not fear this time, but desire, basic and primal.

Suddenly she wanted more than anything to see his eyes, to eliminate the barrier that hid his gaze from her. That shielded his stare. That masked whatever emotion he might have been feeling at that moment.

As though sensing her intentions, he moved away from her sharply, as if she had burned him. "Let's go," he said, his voice flat and cold.

In a flash, just like that, the moment became only a memory. Or an illusion, Erin thought, surprised at the regret she felt. "I haven't talked to Gerard," she protested.

"There's no one here," he said. "You're wasting your time." Then he strode past her toward the street.

Erin hurried to follow him out of the alley. She

caught up with him at the street. "Have you talked to Gerard?" she persisted.

His gaze scanned the darkening sky, but he said nothing.

"Look, you might as well answer my questions," she said angrily. "I'm not going away until you do."

He started walking down the street toward his car.

"I'm sure you've made the connection in all this," she called after him. "I'm sure you don't need me to tell you what it is."

He kept walking.

"It's vampires," she said. A man passing by on the street gazed at her in shock. Then he hurried his steps.

But Slade's stride never slowed. He said over his shoulder, "Sounds like you're starting to believe your own stories."

Exasperated, Erin started up the street after him. "Surely you have to realize it's more than a coincidence that I write books about vampires, my sister was cast in a play about one, and then she turns up dead, all the blood..." Erin trailed off, unable to finish. Every time she thought about what had happened to Megan, the world around her began spinning madly out of control. When she thought about what she was saying, what she was actually thinking...

Slade stopped and turned so swiftly Erin had to dig her heels into the pavement to keep from plowing into him. His scarred hands reached out and grabbed her shoulders. "Just what the hell are you trying to say, Erin? That you believe in vampires? That you think one killed your sister? Where is she then? Why isn't she one?" he taunted.

Erin swallowed hard. "I'm not saying I actually believe in vampires. I'm saying someone who thinks he's a vampire might have killed Megan. Someone who read my books or saw her in Gerard's play. Someone with a twisted mind who can't distinguish fantasy from reality."

"There's only one problem with that theory. Gerard's play hasn't opened yet."

"I know, but there have been plenty of rehearsals, and there are dozens of people connected with the play, including Gerard. That's exactly why I wanted to talk to him."

"And that's exactly why you shouldn't," he warned grimly. He ran a hand through his short, dark hair, as if suddenly weary of the conversation. "Come on," he said, "I'll drive you home."

Erin shivered inside her coat. Twilight had fallen in earnest while they stood talking. She didn't relish walking home in the dark, but neither could she accept Slade's offer, obviously made out of some misplaced sense of obligation. "Thanks, but I don't like to be indebted," she said tersely. "To anyone."

He turned his head toward her. "What do you think I'd demand in restitution? Your soul?" For a long moment, they stared at each other in silence. Then he opened the door of his car, and without another word, Erin slid inside.

His car was a little like riding in a bullet, she decided. Low and lean and fast as lightning. The close confines made her even more aware of the man sitting beside her. She sneaked a glance at his rigid profile. He turned his head slowly, and she found herself captured by his shielded gaze.

"So tell me how you came to be a horror writer."

Erin raised a brow at his tone. "You mean, how does someone like me dream up stories about vampires? Not to mention werewolves and ghosts and other things that go bump in the night?"

"Something like that."

"My therapist suggested I try it. For my own good, of course."

One brow tilted above his glasses. "What kind of therapy made you become a horror writer?" The trace of irony in his tone made Erin smile.

"I guess it does sound a little strange. I've always been plagued by nightmares, ever since Megan and I were kids. My mother used to leave us alone at night a lot. Sometimes she wouldn't come back for several days. She would warn us before she left that there were monsters living in the basement, waiting to grab us if we left the apartment.

"Over the years, those nightmares sometimes became real to me. I couldn't always tell when I was dreaming or…hallucinating." Erin's fingers twisted together in her lap, and she stared down at them, remembering. "Dr. Lancaster thought it might help if I wrote down the dreams when I had them. She thought it would help keep them in the realm of fantasy for me. And that's how my writing career got started."

"You actually dream the things you write about?" He didn't sound pleased. "Your mother did that to you?"

"I don't suppose she would have won any parent-of-the-year awards," Erin tried to quip, but her light tone fell flat. The truth was, she'd never been able to find any lightness in her past at all. Only darkness and shadows and endless, endless fear. "One night when I was eight and Megan was four, Mother left the apartment and she never came back."

"What happened?"

Erin shrugged. "We never found out. Megan and I were alone in that apartment for almost three weeks before...well, before we made our presence known to anyone."

Megan had gotten really sick, Erin remembered. They'd been out of food for days, and Megan had been so weak she could hardly get out of bed. Erin's fear for her sister's health had finally outweighed her terror of the monsters in the basement. She'd gone downstairs to a neighbor's apartment and knocked on the door. She could still picture Mrs. Cooper's appalled expression when she'd followed Erin back up to their apartment.

"Did the police look for your mother?" Slade asked quietly.

"They said they did." Erin winced at the undisguised bitterness in her voice. She took a deep breath, feeling Slade's eyes on her in the darkness.

"Is that why you don't trust the police?"

"Partly." She shrugged, looking out the window. Then she turned her gaze to meet his. "And partly because I just don't trust anyone."

"Wise move," he said, so softly Erin wondered if she'd heard him correctly. "What happened to you and Megan after that?"

"An aunt moved in with us. She had some money from a divorce settlement, and Megan and I owned the apartment so the three of us managed okay. She died the year I graduated high school." Erin had been planning to leave New York then, but because she couldn't leave Megan alone and Megan didn't want to leave New York, she'd stayed on, going to college at NYU until Megan finished high school. Then she'd left in spite of Megan's pleas.

"Tough life," Slade said grimly.

"It had its moments," Erin agreed. "But I expect you've seen worse."

"Meaning?"

"You know...being a cop." Erin made a vague gesture with her hand. "Dealing with criminals. Tracking down murderers. Chasing thugs through dark alleys. Don't tell me, it's all part of the job, right? You get used to it.''

"Not entirely."

"But you do it, anyway. Day in and day out. You could quit, you know."

He slowed for a traffic light. "No," he said. "I couldn't."

"Why not?"

Erin thought at first he wasn't going to answer her, then he shrugged, his foot coming down heavy on the accelerator as the light changed. The car shot forward into the night. "This job is part of me now. It's who I am."

"What you do is who you are?" Erin shook her head in derision. "I read that somewhere once, but I don't buy it."

"Don't you?" His tone was caustic as he spared her a glance. "Can you separate yourself from your writing? You said yourself your books are a part of you."

"That's different."

"Yeah. It usually is."

"No, I mean it," she insisted. "When you write, you *have* to put yourself in your stories. You *have* to draw on your own background, pour in your own emotions, because what else is there? But being a cop—"

"Is different," he finished dryly. "We should be able to separate ourselves from our jobs. Who we are shouldn't affect what we do, and what we do shouldn't affect who we are. We shouldn't have emotions at all, right?''

''I didn't mean it that way,'' Erin defended.

Pulling over to the curb in front of her apartment building, he shut off the engine and turned toward her in the dark. ''Well, for whatever it's worth, I happen to agree with you. Someone in my line of work shouldn't have emotions.''

''Are you saying you don't?'' There was a faint challenge in her tone.

''I'm saying I can't afford to. I can't afford to have anything more—or deeper—than basic instincts.'' A streetlight cast deep shadows in the car, making him seem even more mysterious. More dangerous. One of his arms curled around the back of her seat. He didn't touch her, but he might as well have. The skin at the back of Erin's neck prickled with awareness, with excitement. He leaned slightly toward her, and she could see herself reflected in his glasses. Her eyes looked large and frightened, like a deer's caught in headlights.

''Like the instinct for survival?'' she asked with a strange little catch in her voice.

''Or hunger. That's about as basic—and instinctive—as you can get.''

Was he talking about food? Or something more primal, more carnal? Like sex without emotion? Was this his subtle way of telling her that he felt the attraction between them, too, and wanted to act on it, but only if she understood the consequences?

There was a slight movement in her hair as his hand moved along the seat, and a bolt of pure sensation shot through her. It was a brief touch so soft she might well have imagined it except for the shivers racing up and down her spine. Except for the rippling disturbance in the pit of her stomach. Except for the delicious tingling where he'd touched her...

"I should go in," she said.

"Yes," he agreed. "You should."

But still she lingered, unwilling to break the tension crackling in the air between them. For the first time in her life, Erin felt alive. Nerve-shattering, mind-whirling, heart-poundingly alive.

The sensations flying through her were both terrifying and thrilling. It was like being on a roller coaster. She found the coward in herself wishing the ride was over before it ever started, even as she discovered the adventuress inside her praying it would never end.

Nicholas Slade made her want what she had never experienced before. He made her desire the things that frightened her the most.

He was so close she could smell the night wind on his clothes, could see the small bruise on his right temple where she'd hit him with her purse. She had the almost irresistible urge to touch it with her fingertips, to soothe it with her lips.

"I really should go in," she said softly.

"I know," he agreed again.

But they both knew she wasn't going to. Erin had been waiting for this from the first moment she'd laid eyes on him. She'd been waiting all her life, she realized now.

Her breath caught in her throat as his hand closed around the back of her neck, and he brought her mouth to his.

It was not like any first kiss she'd ever experienced. Not even like one she might have dreamed of. The moment his lips touched hers, a whole new world opened for Erin, a world of secrets and whispers. A world that had once terrified her as she'd hovered on the rim, but now, plunging in, Erin realized for the first time just how mesmerizing the night could be. What a breathtaking trip through the darkness a man like Nicholas Slade could take her on.

His lips stroked hers, teasing them open until Erin felt deliciously vulnerable to him. She parted her lips even wider, and he needed no further invitation. His tongue explored the intimate recesses of her mouth, sending thrill after thrill skimming over Erin's body. She shivered as his hand slipped inside her coat to caress the tender flesh at her throat.

His mouth released hers to trace the line of her jaw, then moved downward, searching. Erin felt the warm, moist kiss against her racing pulse, and her eyes fluttered closed at the exquisite sensations that had been set in motion inside her. She moaned softly, craving more.

"Your skin is like silk," he murmured, his breath hot beneath her ear. His hand was stroking her neck again, making her tremble with anticipation. There was something so darkly erotic about the way he kissed her, about the way he caressed her. It was as if there were emotions contained within him that he could barely keep leashed. Erin wanted them unleashed. She wanted him to kiss her again with all the intensity she knew simmered just beneath the surface of his grim facade.

She wanted him to sweep her up into his arms, to carry her inside to her apartment, to lie down beside her on the bed. Then she wanted him to...

What was happening to her, she thought fleetingly. What power did he have over her? What kind of spell had he cast that made her want him so? That made her crave the dark, passionate, erotic lovemaking she knew he would be capable of?

"Nick," she whispered, testing his name for the first time. "You do such strange things to me. I've never known anyone like you."

"Pray you never do again," he said, pulling back to stare into her eyes. His shielded gaze drew her like a magnet. Erin couldn't seem to look away. He fascinated her, frightened her, made her wish her forbidden fantasies could come true. "If you knew what was good for you," he warned, "you would leave this city and never look back."

"Is that what you want?"

"What I want," he said almost savagely, "isn't an issue here. I'm trying to do what's best for you. What's right."

"What's right is for me to help you find Megan's killer," Erin said.

His fingers touched her face again, almost against his will. "You make it hard to say no," he said. "You make me want—"

*What I've always feared the most,* Erin thought.

"I have to go," he said abruptly, cutting himself off. "There's someone I have to meet."

"Is it about the case?"

He hesitated, then said, "Yes. But I can't take you with me. Not where I'm going."

"Will you call me if you find out anything?"

"I'll call you," he said in a voice that sounded oddly resigned. "I don't think I have any choice now."

# CHAPTER SIX

He'd let her help in the investigation because he had no choice now, Slade thought as he headed toward the river. Because it was the only way to make sure she remained safe. Because it was the only way to make certain that she didn't find out too much.

But there would be a price to pay, he thought grimly, remembering the passion of their kiss. One hell of a price. The longer he stayed around Erin Ramsey, the harder it would be to keep his hands off her. The harder it would be to keep reminding himself that there was no way someone like him could have someone like her. She was fighting her own demons. She sure as hell didn't need his.

He parked the car and got out. As he walked the darkened streets near the river, a mist blew in from the water and curled with the steam that rose from the sidewalk grates. In the maze of crumbling warehouses and shadowy streets, a body could remain hidden forever.

The perfect place for a predator's lair, he thought, feeling the hair at the back of his neck rise in warning. He could be walking into a trap, he realized, but he also knew he had to see if Christina Harris was here or not. He had to make sure she was safe.

He paused at the mouth of the alley near Nosferatu's. There was no sign of her. He hoped to hell she'd changed her mind. Hoped she'd had more sense than to come back here. What could she possibly know about Megan Ramsey's killer? he thought, fighting the same black premonition he'd experienced the night Megan Ramsey had died.

Closing his eyes, he let the seductive night scents drift over him. He could smell the river, but beneath that, more subtly, came the unmistakable tang of blood. Slade's pulse quickened.

Across the street a derelict noisily rummaged through a Dumpster, but Slade ignored him. What he listened for now were far more discriminating sounds. A contented sigh. An erotic moan. The frenzied suckling of an insatiable mouth.

Slowly, still watching the shadows, Slade entered the alley. It was cold in the inky darkness. He pulled the collar of his coat around his neck as his gaze combed the garbage-strewn gutters. A rat scurried across the broken pavement in front of him and dissolved into the shadows. Slade saw the tiny eyes gleam as they watched him expectantly.

The smell of blood clung to the air now, heavy and sweet as syrup. The skin at the back of his neck prickled with warning again. Slade moved through the thick shadows. The scars on his hand throbbed as his fist closed over the weapon he carried in his coat pocket.

"Christina?" he whispered and peered through the darkness, using the night vision that seemed more curse than gift.

And then he saw the body. Not Christina, he realized, but an old man. One of the city's homeless who was too easily preyed upon by the denizens of darkness. He turned the man's head to locate the puncture wounds in his neck. They were no longer bleeding. The man was dead. He'd have to be taken care of before—

Slade sensed her presence before he saw her. Slowly he stood, watching the mist and steam writhe and curl as she came toward him out of the deepest gloom of the alley. Her blond hair shimmered in the moonlight, and her dimples marked the sweetness of her smile.

"Christina." Slade felt an almost overwhelming sense of relief at first, then a dawning horror as he saw her eyes for the first time. The light blue had deepened to silver, and in the dimness of the alley they glowed with a bestial fire.

She lifted a hand toward him. "Help me, Nick. You promised, remember?"

She looked very young, her face smooth, her red lips beguiling. But the innocence that Slade had always admired, that he had tried to save, was gone. She was soulless now. Evil.

And someone had made her lure him here to witness her transformation. To make him do what would have to be done to her. Slade knew what to expect. He knew what he had to do. But that didn't make it any easier. He felt sickened by the sight of her, by the loss of another's life.

"Nick. You promised you'd help me, remember? You promised to protect me." Her voice tore at his soul. With all he knew, Slade still had to fight the urge to go to her. Her voice was compelling, her eyes—those glowing eyes—hypnotic.

"Why didn't you listen to me?" he said in an angry voice. "Why did you come back here?"

"Don't be mad." She continued walking toward him, her arms outstretched to him, beseeching him. "I need you. I'm so cold. Please help me. You promised you'd help me."

Don't look at her! he commanded himself. Don't listen to her!

He knew the rules. He knew what had to be done, but she looked so young and so beautiful. She reminded him of Simone.

"I'll help you," he said, focusing his gaze away from her mesmerizing stare. "I'll help you, Christina."

"I've always liked you, Nick," she was saying. "I've always wondered what it would be like to be kissed by you. Kiss me, Nick. Please…just once…"

She was smiling at him, and for a moment Slade let his gaze drift back to her mouth. Something gleamed in the darkness, and he knew that her teeth were growing longer, sharper, preparing for the kill. "Nick," she whispered. "Just a little closer."

"Who did this to you?" he asked as she moved slowly toward him, seemingly gliding on air, no longer earthbound.

"Don't you know?"

*I'll see you in hell, Slade.*

The voice in his head was so powerful, so intense, that for an instant Slade's guard was lowered. Christina's cold touch brought him back. Already she was upon him. He couldn't afford to let his mind wander. He knew that. But...

Her fingers fluttered against his face, and Slade shuddered. Her lips curled back, revealing her fangs. She lifted her head toward his neck.

Slade moved the stake between them, and the moment Christina lowered her mouth to his neck, he plunged it through her heart with all his might. She staggered back, clutching at the stake, trying to withdraw it from her body. Her features contorted, revealing her horror and pain, but she didn't make a sound. She didn't have to. Slade heard the echo of a thousand screams inside his own head.

She fell to the ground, and he knelt beside her, cradling her slight body in his arms. Her eyes were closed, and he saw that it was only with a great deal of effort that she managed to open them. They were clear blue again. Sweet and innocent.

"Nick," she whispered. "Thank you, Nick." And then her eyes closed for the last time.

Slade staggered to his feet. His whole body was shaking as he made his way back to the old man's body. Quickly he repeated what he'd done to Christina, then rose and stumbled out of the alley.

He paused for a moment, leaning against the side of a building as he fought the darkness washing over him. Images raced through his mind. Screams and pleas filled his head. Visions of blood, warm and flowing, flooded through his mind, and he was only dimly aware of the scream of sirens in the distance.

He had warned Megan Ramsey away from the darkness, and she was dead. He had warned Christina Harris, and now she was dead, too. That was what she had meant when she said she couldn't afford to be seen with him.

Who would be next? he thought in dawning horror. Who would die next because of him?

Suddenly an image of Erin's face floated through his mind. She was looking up at him with those eyes that looked like violets and those lips that looked so soft and tender and sweet. She was more beautiful and more desirable than any other woman he'd ever known before.

And at that moment he knew he would do anything to save her from the darkness that had claimed Simone and Megan and now Christina. He would do anything to protect her, but what if he couldn't? What if he failed her as he had all the others?

*I'll see you in hell, Slade.*

"You're dead," Slade muttered aloud, but the cold black premonition wouldn't go away.

The sirens grew louder as two police cars screeched to a halt in front of the alley. Slade watched the officers emerge, weapons drawn, as they headed across the street toward him. Then he turned and without a word melted back into the shadows.

If he stayed, there would be questions he couldn't answer. Questions that would arouse old suspicions. Questions that could put him in the limelight once more. He didn't want to go through that kind of scrutiny again, not now. Not when there was so much to hide.

But more than that, he knew he had to remain free to hunt the darkness, to stalk the evil that now stalked him.

Erin spent a sleepless night. She kept hearing noises in the apartment, kept hearing the pipes banging in the basement, and she remembered that as a child she had always thought the monsters in the basement were creating that sound just to torment her, just to let her know that they were down there waiting for her.

She kept thinking about Nick. About how he had kissed her and how she had wanted him to. Time and again she relived the thrill of the moment when his lips had first touched hers.

She couldn't get involved with him. She knew that. Apart from the ethical question of the case, Erin had long ago resolved to live her life alone. There were too many unanswered questions in her life, too many unresolved issues from her past. She'd learned the hard way that dragging all that baggage into a relationship could only end in disaster, in more heartache. Better just to live her life alone.

But sometimes…sometimes in the dead of night, when she grew weary of fighting her demons, Erin wondered what it would be like to share her life with someone who understood about nightmares. What would it be like to turn to someone special and have him hold her in his arms until the sun came up. Sometimes she couldn't help wondering what it would be like to be loved. Really loved…

At dawn she finally dozed off. It was late when she woke up, and she hurriedly showered and dressed. She had a lot to do today. In spite of Nick's warnings, Erin had every intention of tracing the last few days of her sister's life, to put at least one demon in her life to rest.

So, for the next few days, Erin walked the streets that Megan had walked, visited the clothing stores where Megan had shopped, browsed through the music stores she knew Megan had frequented. She immersed herself in Megan's life, storing up bits and pieces of information that she knew might somehow be important in completing the picture of her sister's life.

And at night she sat alone in the apartment, waiting for dawn, waiting for Nick to call. But he didn't.

By day, Erin continued her mission. Several of the salespersons in the shops recognized her immediately, mistaking her for Megan. The first time it happened, Erin had been disturbed, then strangely excited. If people mistook her for Megan, they might let slip a clue, a hint that could help bring her sister's murderer to justice.

As Erin walked home one afternoon, the sights and sounds of the city assailed her senses. Rock music blared from boom boxes in Washington Square, and the crowded little cafés and bistros overflowed onto the streets with the first wave of well-dressed young men and women winding down after a hectic day on Wall Street. It was a pleasant scene, typical and un-threatening.

Yet in the fading light of day, Erin experienced a funny feeling in the pit of her stomach. Some omen warned her things were not always what they seemed.

"Erin? Is that you? Erin, wait up!"

It took a moment for the voice to register. Erin half turned to see Racine DiMeneci striding across the street toward her. Racine wore a black wool cape that swirled around her in the wind, and in the late-afternoon sunlight, her hair blazed like fire.

She eyed Erin speculatively as she fell into step beside her. "I thought it was you, but…you look different today," she said uncertainly. "It's your hair. You're wearing it down, like Megan used to."

Erin self-consciously fingered the windblown curls. "I didn't have time to put it up," she said. "How are you, Racine?"

Racine shook her head, frowning. "It's amazing," she said, ignoring Erin's question. "The resemblance was always striking, but now it's…it's positively uncanny. I thought for a moment when I first saw you that you *were* Megan. Isn't that her coat?"

Was that suspicion Erin heard in her voice? Just the barest hint of accusation? "I didn't bring anything heavy enough for this weather," Erin said defensively. "It was eighty degrees when I left Los Angeles."

"Novembers in New York can be hell," Racine agreed absently. She paused, then said, "I couldn't help noticing that Detective Slade brought you home a few nights ago."

Erin felt the pulse in her throat give a little leap at the mention of his name. Ever since that night she'd been trying to keep at bay memories of his kiss, but with little success. Even now she felt her face grow warm as his image materialized in her mind. She saw the dark way he'd looked at her just before he kissed her, and her blood raced. She took a deep breath, willing away the unfamiliar sensations Nick's kiss had released inside her, the disappointment that he hadn't called her since. It was almost as if he was avoiding her, she thought.

Racine's voice cut into her thoughts. "Any news on the investigation?"

"I'm afraid not."

"Does that mean you'll be going back to L.A., then?" Out of the corner of her eye, Erin saw Racine slant her an anxious glance.

"I haven't made any immediate plans," Erin said with a shrug. "There's still a lot to be done here. I'm sure you understand."

"Of course." But Racine didn't sound too sure. She took Erin's arm and pulled her to a stop.

Erin turned to face her in surprise. "What's the matter?"

Racine looked distressed. "I'm afraid you'll think I'm butting in where I have no business."

"Is this about the case?" Erin asked sharply.

"In a way. It's about Detective Slade."

Erin's heart sped up again. Had Racine seen them that night? Had she witnessed their kiss? "What about him?"

Racine chewed her lip, obviously embarrassed. "I couldn't help seeing you the other night," she confirmed. "I wasn't trying to spy on you, honest I wasn't, but his car was parked right out front and I...well..."

"It's okay," Erin murmured.

"No, it isn't. I mean, it isn't okay that you were with him. Oh, God, I'm babbling," she said, rolling her eyes heavenward. "I never babble. It's just…"

"What?"

"I'm worried about you, Erin. I don't think you should let yourself get too close to that man. To Slade."

Erin stared at her. "Why?"

"Because I don't trust him," Racine said. "I can't explain it. Maybe it's just those dark glasses he wears all the time, but for some reason I keep thinking that I know him from somewhere."

Erin remained silent. Racine's words had echoed an uneasiness already simmering inside her. She wasn't completely sure she trusted Nick, either, but for some reason, Racine's warning annoyed her. She said coolly, "You don't have to worry about me. I've been on my own for a long time. I can take care of myself."

Racine's green eyes clouded with worry. She shook her head. "That's just what Megan used to say," she returned. She gripped Erin's arm for a moment longer, then released her. "I have to run now, Erin, but please think about what I said. There's something very unnatural about a man who keeps his eyes covered from the world. It makes me wonder what he's trying to hide."

Erin stood for a moment, watching Racine disappear into the crowd on the street.

*"It makes me wonder what he's trying to hide."*

If Erin was truthful with herself, she would have to admit that she'd wondered the same thing. She thought about the scars on his hands and wondered if perhaps his eyes had been scarred, too. Perhaps he was self-conscious about the way he looked? But there was certainly no need to be. Erin had never met a man so darkly attractive in her life. She'd never known anyone who had affected her so deeply. The scars on his hands were far from repulsive to her. They seemed like an affirmation of life. They seemed strong and capable and oddly comforting.

Across the street, the colorful wares of a flower vendor caught her eye, and Erin expertly dodged through the traffic, ignoring the blast of horns as though she'd never been away from the city's traffic.

The old woman tending the open-air stall was wearing a faded purple skirt and an NYU sweatshirt. She beamed a ragged smile as Erin browsed through the flowers. "How did the roses do, hon?"

"I beg your pardon?"

"The roses you bought last Friday," the old woman said. "The red ones."

Erin realized that the flower lady, like so many other people that day, was mistaking her for Megan. Then she realized something else. Her sister had bought roses on the day she'd been murdered. If Erin hadn't been dressed the way she was dressed, she never would have learned that information.

"They died," she murmured, selecting another dozen roses and fishing in her purse for the correct change.

The woman shook her head sadly as she accepted Erin's money. "For all their beauty, roses are very delicate, you know. They just don't seem to last long enough, do they?"

Erin made a noncommittal reply and retraced her steps across the street, heading toward home. The sun had set now, and the chill of twilight settled around her. She hurried her pace, wanting to get inside before dark. Shadows were already falling across the street, casting the whole neighborhood in an aura of deep gloom.

The back of her neck prickled in a now-familiar way. Erin turned and hastily scanned the street, but nothing seemed amiss. Darkness was falling quickly, reason enough for her uneasiness. She shivered, then ran up the stairs of the apartment building and stepped quickly inside.

The hallway lay in deep shade. Erin paused, catching her breath before making the climb to Megan's apartment. Almost inadvertently her gaze strayed to the basement staircase. There was an apartment below, but she didn't know if it was occupied or not. Years ago it had always remained vacant. "Only monsters live there," she heard Desiree whisper in her mind. "Don't go down there, Erin. They're waiting for you."

As with so many other things, both Erin and Megan had always been terrified of that basement, but wasn't that one of the reasons she'd come back here? To face the monsters from her past?

Erin set her packages down in the hallway and took a cautious step toward the top of the stairs. For a long moment, she stood staring down into the almost complete blackness. Go on, she urged herself. Prove to yourself once and for all that Desiree was wrong. There's nothing to be afraid of down there.

She put a hand on the railing and stepped down. The stair creaked, sending a chill up her spine. "Coward," she muttered, descending a few steps more. Near the bottom she paused, letting her eyes adjust to the darkness. Several discarded boxes were stacked against a wall, and to the left of the staircase, a door stood slightly ajar. The air smelled musty and dank, and a slight breeze fluttered Erin's hair, as if a window stood open somewhere. The door moved slightly, and Erin jumped. Then something brushed against her ankle, and she very nearly had a heart attack.

She felt the softness again, then heard a *meow*. Erin let out a shaky laugh. The cat's eyes glowed in the dark as it gazed up plaintively at Erin, reminding her chillingly of the eyes she'd seen the night Megan died.

"You almost sent me to an early grave," she admonished, and the cat meowed again. Erin bent and tentatively stroked the silky fur. The cat relaxed for a moment under her ministrations, but suddenly the hair on its back stood on end as its head shot up. Then, before Erin could react, a razor-sharp claw shot out and scratched the back of her hand. Like an arrow, the cat flew past her and disappeared somewhere in the darkness beneath the stairs.

Erin cried out at the sharp sting on her hand, automatically lifting it to her mouth. Then her arm froze in midair as she heard a faint sound coming from the other side of the door. She stood dead still, listening to the whispers of movement, as if something—or someone—was stirring about inside.

Probably rats, she told herself, but a heavy sense of unease assailed her. Perhaps she wasn't as ready to face the monsters as she'd thought.

Nursing her bleeding hand, Erin turned to flee, but someone stood at the top of the stairs, completely blocking her path.

# CHAPTER SEVEN

He had the most uncanny ability to materialize from thin air, Erin thought fleetingly. To appear suddenly with the darkness.

"Erin?"

Her heart began to pound even harder at the sound of Slade's voice. Slowly she mounted the stairs toward him. Through the glass door behind him, Erin saw that night had fallen in earnest since she'd come in, and once again she thought how very much a part of the night he seemed. The dark glasses, the leather coat, the grim expression—all created an air of mystery, of danger. Erin shivered again, just watching him, the memory of his kiss coming back to her. Along with the fact that he hadn't called her in three days.

She brushed by him and bent to pick up her packages. The roses already looked a little droopy, she noticed absently.

"What were you doing down there?" Slade asked when she turned back to face him.

"I heard a noise," Erin said.

"So you went to check it out?" His voice was grim, his expression even more dangerous. "And what if it had been the murderer down there, waiting for you?''

*"Don't go down there, Erin. They're waiting for you."*

She shrugged off Slade's hand. "There was nothing waiting for me down there but a bad-tempered cat," she said, lifting her hand up to inspect the scratch.

"Let me see that." His hand shot out and captured hers. Beads of blood dotted the skin, but the sting of the scratch receded against the warmth of his touch. "You'd better put something on it," he said, dropping her hand abruptly as if he, too, had felt the heat.

"I was just about to. Was there something you wanted to talk to me about?" He didn't look pleased to see her, Erin thought. Behind his dark glasses, she knew he was frowning at her.

"Why are you dressed like that?"

Erin's hand reflexively flew to her loosened hair. "Like...what?"

"Like your sister."

"How would you know how Megan dressed?" Erin asked quickly. He didn't say a word at first, merely stared at her, and then Erin realized that he'd seen Megan's body after she'd died. Perhaps he didn't want to remind her of that night. She turned and started up the stairway. "You'd be surprised how many people have mistaken me for her in the past few days."

"Is that what you want?" He followed her up the stairs.

She glanced at him over her shoulder as she unlocked the door. "It can be useful."

"In what way?"

"In tracing the last days of Megan's life." She turned to face him, her chin lifted in defiance. But his response took her totally off guard.

"That's what I want to talk to you about. I think it's time we started working together."

Erin's jaw dropped. "Are you serious?"

"Dead serious."

"Then why haven't you called me?" Erin hated the way her voice sounded. Her accusation sounded more personal than professional, and that was the last thing she wanted him to think. "Why haven't you kept me informed?"

"That's what I'm here to do now," he said.

Erin turned and pushed open the door of the apartment, flipped on the light and set the roses down on the bar that separated the kitchen and living room. She closed the door behind her and carried the remaining packages into the hallway. "I'll be right back," she said.

Leaving her coat in the bedroom, she located Megan's first-aid kit in the bathroom, then liberally dosed the scratch with antiseptic. As she was putting away the supplies, she caught a glimpse of herself in the mirror. Touching the loose curls at her shoulders, she turned first one way and then the other. It really was amazing how different she looked with her hair down, how much she looked like Megan.

She studied her reflection in the mirror. The black rayon dress she wore swirled around her ankles, and the neckline left her throat and neck completely bare.

*Yes, that's better.*

Erin paused as the voice fluttered through her mind. She turned, glancing around the room. "Megan?" The only sound was a soft rustle as the curtains at the window stirred slightly in the breeze.

Slade was standing at the mantel, gazing at the pictures of Erin and Megan when Erin came back into the living room. His head turned toward her, and she knew he was watching her intently as she crossed the room, carrying the vase she'd found in Megan's room. He held one of the pictures in his hand. It was the one of Erin and Megan and their mother.

"When was this taken?" he asked.

Erin resisted the urge to reach out and snatch the picture from his hand. It was too revealing. She hadn't yet learned to hide her fear. "I was eight and Megan was four," she said. "It was taken two days before our mother...disappeared."

"She was very beautiful," he said, watching her.

"Yes, she was."

"You look like her."

She was surprised by the compliment. Her heart

fluttered inside her chest. "I hope that's where the resemblance ends," she tried to say lightly.

"I'm sure of it." His voice was surprisingly gentle. He returned the picture to the mantel, but before his hand moved away, Erin saw one of his long, thin fingers stroke her image in the photo. It was an oddly compassionate gesture, and the effect on Erin was immediate.

She turned and walked quickly away from him, her heart thumping against her chest. Better not get too close, she advised herself. Better not want his compassion.

Her hands were trembling slightly as she picked up the roses and walked around the bar to the kitchen, arranging the flowers in a vase. Slade walked across the room and stood on the other side of the bar, watching her. "Roses don't suit you," he said flatly.

Erin glanced up. "They were Megan's favorite. In fact, one of the things I learned today was that she bought roses the day she died." Erin's voice faltered. She busied herself, putting water in the vase until she was sure she had her emotions under control. Then she walked over and set the vase in the center of the dining room table, at the end of the bar, replacing the wilted ones.

"What else did you learn?"

"I learned that she always dressed in black, at least toward the end. That seems to tie in with her obsession with...vampires," Erin said hesitantly.

The room grew silent. Erin stared down at the roses. "I know you think I'm crazy," she said. "I know you don't believe in vampires."

"And you do?"

"I...think Megan did. I think that's why she went to the club Racine told us about. I think we should go there, too, Nick."

His reaction was immediate. His expression darkened. "I'll take care of that place. I don't want you anywhere near it."

"But you said it was time we worked together. You want me to tell you everything I learn, but you don't want to give me anything in return, is that it?"

"I'm willing to share information with you," Slade said. "I'm just not willing to risk your life."

He stared her down until Erin was forced to look away. "Tell me what you came here to tell me," she said a little testily.

Slade gazed around the apartment as if feeling the chill of memories, sensing the ghosts from Erin's past. "Not here," he said. "Let's grab a bite to eat somewhere."

"Aren't you on duty?"

"This is business," he said.

Business not pleasure, Erin thought, feeling unaccountably disappointed. He couldn't have made himself clearer. "I'll get my coat and we can go then."

He took her to a small restaurant only a few blocks away from the apartment. Rubinoff's Deli was the kind of neighborhood eatery that New York was famous for. Bells over the door tinkled melodiously as Slade and Erin stepped inside, and the delicious aroma of freshly baked bread, accompanied by the more pungent scent of garlic, permeated the air. Red-and-white-checked tablecloths adorned the half-dozen tables near the rear and candles flickering in fat red jars chased away the gloomy twilight and gave the place a homey, intimate atmosphere.

Behind a long glass counter, a heavyset man with thick black hair salted with gray stirred a huge, steaming pot of soup. His swarthy face, red and glistening from the hot stove, lit up when he spotted Slade. "Nicholas! I don't believe my eyes! Where've you been hiding all this time?" He wiped his beefy hands on the white apron slung around his neck as he hurried around the counter to clap Slade on the back. "You been working too hard, eh, Nicholas?"

"You know how it is," Slade responded noncommittally, steering Erin past the overflowing shelves of bottled delicacies toward a secluded booth in the back.

"Yeah, I know how it is," Mr. Rubinoff agreed as he followed on their heels. His gaze frankly appraised Erin as she slid onto the red vinyl booth. "Mama was just saying the other day how much she still misses seeing you. 'Remember how Nicholas used to come by after school when he was a boy, Papa?' she said." His dark, warm gaze included Erin in the conversation. "'Every day, three-thirty, just like clockwork, Nicholas and Simone would come waltzing through that door.'"

Slade's mouth tightened. "That was a long time ago."

"Yeah, a long time ago," Mr. Rubinoff agreed, his smile dimming. "Before you started hiding behind those dark glasses, eh? Before you too busy for your old friends."

"That's not how it is," Slade said, and Erin was amazed at how defensive he sounded. She'd never seen him like this. So...human. "Things change," he muttered.

"Things change," Mr. Rubinoff echoed. "Now Simone's gone and you done moved away." A look of profound sadness passed over the old man's face, making Erin wonder who Simone was. Why had her name evoked such strong reactions from both men?

Mr. Rubinoff's gaze rested on Erin again, and some of the warmth returned to his eyes. "The past is past, though, eh? It's been eight years. Time to move on. The important thing is that you've brought another pretty girl to see me today."

The way Mr. Rubinoff was looking at her, beaming first at her and then Slade, made Erin's face heat with color. She knew that Slade was looking at her, too, and that made her heart beat even faster.

"This is Erin," Slade said. "Erin Ramsey. She and

I are here to discuss a case I'm working on," he added pointedly.

Mr. Rubinoff took the hint. "Fine," he said, throwing up his hands. "I bring you two plates of Stroganoff and a bottle of my best Romanian wine to enjoy while you talk."

"I take it you and Mr. Rubinoff are old friends," Erin said after the old man had hurried off.

Slade shrugged. "My mother used to work here before she remarried and moved south. She and I lived in a little apartment over the restaurant. The Rubinoffs were like my grandparents. They took an interest in everything I did."

Erin wanted to ask him about the girl Mr. Rubinoff had mentioned, but something held her back. Slade's hands were resting on the table, and he was gazing down at them in a way that made Erin wonder if he was the one now being haunted by ghosts. "What about your father?" she asked, instead.

"He was killed when I was just a kid," Slade said. "He was a cop."

Somehow that information surprised Erin. He seemed like such a loner to her. It was difficult to think of him having a family, a mother who had remarried and a dead father in whose footsteps he'd followed.

Nick's just a man, Erin thought. And, like everyone else, he'd been hurt. Perhaps that explained why she'd been so drawn to him from the first, why the kinship between them seemed even stronger tonight. It wasn't just the physical attraction, Erin admitted reluctantly. It was deeper than that. More profound. And much more dangerous.

She felt Nick's eyes on her again, and she averted her gaze.

Mr. Rubinoff came back with steaming plates and, with a flourish, poured the wine, then waited patiently while Erin sampled them both. "Delicious," she said, and meant it. The food and wine were just what she'd needed, she realized, not to mention the comfortable atmosphere of the deli.

She began to relax. The apartment, with all its memories, seemed a long way away from this cheerful place, and she was grateful to Nick for bringing her here, for letting her share in this warmth. For a while, they ate in silence. But then, when they were both finished, Erin knew she couldn't put off the inevitable any longer. She toyed with her wineglass as she gazed at him across the flickering candle. "What have you found out, Nick?"

He hesitated, then said, "Two bodies were found in an alley down by the river a few nights ago."

Erin's hand jerked, upsetting her wine. Slade's hand shot out and righted the glass, and for a moment, their fingers brushed. Erin fought the urge to cling to his hand. The warmth from the food and wine suddenly left her. The comfort of the deli fled. "Who were they?"

"The young woman has been identified as Christina Harris. The other one was an old man. A John Doe."

"What's the connection with Megan?" Erin asked anxiously. "I assume there is one. That's why we're here, isn't it?"

Slade's mouth tightened. "There were marks on both their necks. Puncture wounds."

Erin felt her breath desert her. "And...the blood...?" She couldn't even finish the question. Slade nodded briefly, and then they both fell silent.

Erin's head reeled. She felt sickened by what she'd heard. She couldn't stand to think that Megan had been killed by such a cold-blooded monster. The thought that her sister might even have known him, loved him—

"Who found the bodies?" she asked suddenly.

"There was an anonymous call to the station. When the officers arrived on the scene, the victims were already dead."

"Did they find anything? Any clues? A motive?" she asked desperately.

"He doesn't need a motive," Slade said roughly. "He kills for pleasure. For sport."

Erin's hands were trembling as she looked up at him. "My God, you talk as if you know him."

"I do," Slade said coldly. "I know him as well as I know myself."

"Then why can't you find him?" she cried. "Why

can't you stop him?'' She was bordering on hysteria, but she couldn't help it. It was terrifying to think that such evil really existed, that her nightmares could really come true. ''You've got to stop him!''

She was clutching his arm, clinging to his hand. His fingers, warm, strong, comforting, closed around hers. ''Take it easy,'' he said softly.

Mr. Rubinoff hurried up to the table. ''Everything okay?'' His worried gaze took in Erin's and Slade's linked hands. Dimly Erin saw what he must have seen—the contrast and the disparity. Nick's hands were huge and strong and hideously scarred. Erin's hands were pale and smooth and flawless. But together they formed a bond. An unbreakable connection. He tightened his hold on her, as if he was reading her thoughts, and for a moment Erin thought she'd glimpsed something in his expression, a flash of emotion behind those dark glasses. Something she hadn't seen in a long, long time. Maybe ever.

''Let's get out of here,'' he said.

Erin's legs were shaking when she stood to comply.

# CHAPTER EIGHT

Slade dropped her off at her apartment, making her promise once again not to open her door to anyone. Erin watched him go with an almost overwhelming feeling of abandonment. He was on duty. She knew he couldn't stay and baby-sit her all night, but the apartment seemed even colder and gloomier after he left. It was hard not to let her imagination run away with her. Hard not to keep going over and over their conversation in her mind.

*"Two bodies were found in an alley down by the river a few nights ago.*

*"There were marks on both their necks. Puncture wounds."*

Don't, Erin thought. Don't think about what that could mean. Don't think about the nightmares you've had and the stories you've written. Don't start thinking they could be true.

But what if they were true? What if a vampire, just like the one in *Demon Lover,* stalked in the darkness out there, was even now searching for his next prey? What if he'd already found his next victim? What if it was her?

The questions echoed off the walls and pounded inside her head. Erin sat on the couch, too scared to even move. Once she and Nick had left the deli, she'd pulled herself together enough to put up a brave front for his benefit, but now that he was gone, the terror closed in on her.

Two more bodies had been found. Dear God, two more people had been murdered. And there were puncture wounds in their necks. Just like Megan. Just like the characters in her book.

*We've been waiting for you, Erin.*

Go back to L.A., she commanded herself. You don't have to stay here. You don't have to prove anything to anyone. Not even to yourself.

Firmly in the grip of panic, Erin jumped up and ran into the bedroom. She grabbed her suitcase and hauled it to the bed, then began flinging her clothes toward it. She *was* going, she thought, almost numbly. She was going and nothing would stop her, but in almost the same instant, her gaze landed on the recorder she'd placed on the dresser earlier that day. Her frantic movements ceased as she stared at the machine.

Erin wasn't sure why it drew her attention, but something compelled her to cross the room and stare down at the recorder, and then suddenly she realized why she felt so uneasy. The recorder was voice activated, and she could see that the tape had been run forward as if it had clicked on in her absence. That could only mean one thing.

Someone had been in the apartment while she was out.

Don't jump to conclusions, she warned herself. Maybe she'd just forgotten to rewind it the last time she'd used it. But Erin was pretty certain that that wasn't the case because she'd checked it out to make sure it was still working after her encounter with Nick in the hallway the day of Megan's funeral. It had been in her purse when she'd hit him. She almost always carried it with her so that any sudden inspiration wouldn't be lost.

Erin took a deep breath. She rewound the tape, then pushed the Play button. The tape started running. At first she couldn't distinguish anything, just a lot of static and what sounded like children singing in the background. She turned up the volume, trying to make out the words, but the sounds were too garbled.

Then, through the static and the chanting came another sound, another voice. Erin gasped, her hand flying to her mouth to stifle a scream as she heard her sister whisper, "Don't leave me, sissy. Not again." It was the voice of a child. The voice of her sister years ago when she had begged Erin to stay with her, to protect her, to save her from the monsters.

And then the recorder clicked off. Erin stood rooted to the spot, her hand clamped to her mouth as her whole body began to shake violently. She remained that way for a long, agonizing moment before she became aware of a new sensation. A new terror. Someone—or something—was watching her.

"Megan?" Erin called out into the silence of the bedroom. At the sound of her voice, the air around her seemed to swirl, to become energized. Erin's hair tingled at the roots as if charged with static electricity. She could feel the current moving through her body, but still she couldn't move. The room grew cold, misty, tomblike. An unnatural fog drifted through the crack at the bottom of the window.

"I'm so cold," a voice whispered through the mist. "Let me in, Erin."

"Megan!" Tears streamed down Erin's face. Her skin was cold and wet, her soul chilled with a premonition she could hardly name. "Dear God, is that you?"

"It's so cold out here. Open the window and let me come in."

Slowly Erin turned her gaze to the second-story window. A face mocked her in the glass. Eyes glowed in the dark as the shadow wavered, seemed to float on nothing but air. Erin screamed and tried to back away, tried to flee that cold, damp room, but something—those eyes—held her in thrall. They gazed, unblinking, straight into her soul.

Beside her the tape recorder turned itself on; the tape ran backward then stopped. The soft click seemed to jolt Erin out of her trance. She stared out the window, seeing only the reflection of her own terrified face.

"This is Slade."

Erin drew a shaky breath. "Nick…"

"Erin? What's wrong?"

"I'm not sure…maybe nothing. I thought I saw something outside my window after you left. You said to call—"

"I'll be right there. Make sure all the windows and doors are bolted."

"But I'm not even sure—"

"Give me ten minutes," he said, and then the phone went dead.

Erin stared at the receiver, unwilling to sever the connection on her end. He'd sounded so calm, so rational. What would he say when he got here and she told him that—

*Dear God.* Erin sat down weakly on the couch, clenching her hands tightly into fists to try to stop the trembling. It *couldn't* have been Megan's voice. Her sister was dead and buried. She couldn't have come back. It wasn't possible. Things like that only happened in Erin's books. The monsters only lived in her dreams. They weren't real. They couldn't be real. And Megan couldn't call to her from the grave.

*Don't leave me, sissy. Not again.*

The pitiful little voice haunted Erin's thoughts. Was she losing her mind? Had she dwelled in the nightmares of her past, lived in the pages of her horror books for so long that she could no longer distinguish between fantasy and reality? Was her guilt pushing her farther and farther into the darkness?

She told herself to get up and check the doors and windows, just as Slade had ordered her to do, but Erin couldn't bring herself to do it. She didn't want to admit how truly terrified she was. Didn't want to give in to that fear, because if she did, if she allowed herself to believe—

The doorbell sounded and Erin's heart jumped. She got up, took a quick look out the window, then went to open the door.

The moment she drew back the door, Slade swore violently. "What the hell do you think you're doing, opening your door without even asking who's on the other side? I could have been the murderer, for all you knew."

Erin took one look at his grim countenance, his dark facade, and silently agreed. He *could* have been the murderer. "I saw your car parked outside," she said.

He didn't bother to respond, but strode into the living room. "What happened?"

Erin closed the door and followed him inside. "It was probably nothing. My imagination..."

When her words trailed away, Slade scowled at her. "Why don't you let me be the judge of that?"

Erin discovered that her legs were still shaking, and

she sat down. His tone suddenly made her want to cry, and she turned her head so he couldn't see her face. "Someone activated my recorder while I was out. I heard…voices…" She faltered, then whispered, "I heard Megan's voice, Nick."

"On the tape recorder?"

"Yes."

"Where is it?"

"In the bedroom," Erin said. "But there's no use trying to play it back. It's been erased."

He stared down at her. "Why did you do that?"

"*I* didn't do it. It…erased all by itself." She pushed her hair from her face with a trembling hand. Before he could respond, she lifted her tortured eyes to his and said, "I know that's impossible. I know I couldn't have seen…what I thought I saw."

"Exactly what did you see?"

She twisted her hands in her lap. "I saw a face in my bedroom window. There aren't any fire escapes outside that window. No balconies, either. But I saw her. *I saw Megan!*"

"That's impossible," Slade said. "You couldn't have. I took care—" He broke off, turned away.

"What do you mean?" Erin said. "What did you start to say?" When he turned around to face her, Erin thought she had never seen an expression so grim, a mouth so harsh. She started to tremble at his look, but she wouldn't let herself look away, wouldn't allow herself to back down. She had to know the truth. All of it. "Tell me!" she cried.

"Megan is dead," he said heavily. "She can't come back, Erin. Believe me. Trust me."

"How can I trust you?" Erin whispered. "I know you're keeping something from me. I know you aren't telling me the complete truth."

"Listen to me," Slade commanded as he sat down beside her. He grabbed her shoulders and turned her to face him. "You need to get out of here. You need to get as far away from this place as fast as you possibly can. There's no reason for you to stay."

"There's every reason to stay," Erin said desperately, wrenching herself away from him. She got up and stood looking down at him. "I can't leave now. I can't leave Megan."

"She's dead, for God's sake! You *can't* help her now."

"But I can," Erin insisted. "Don't you see? I can help her rest in peace. That's what she wants. That's what she needs—"

Slade swore viciously as he jumped to his feet, grabbing her arms as if to shake some sense into her. "Damn it, Erin, nothing's worth putting yourself in this much danger. You have no idea what you're dealing with, what could happen to you. You have no earthly idea...."

"Then tell me," she begged. "Tell me the truth."

His scarred hands fell away from her arms. "Just go. Get the hell away from this city. From me."

"You talk as if you're the murderer," Erin whispered in a raw voice. "You talk as if I should be scared of *you*." Slade spun and walked toward the door without uttering a word. Erin gazed at his back for only a split second before she caught up with him. She clutched his arm. "*Should* I be scared of you? Answer me, damn you."

He stared down at her, and even though Erin still clung to his arm, he suddenly seemed a million miles away from her. "Yes," he said, and Erin thought she had never heard a word sound so bleak, so chilling.

"You're not the murderer," she said in a deceptively calm voice.

"You think I'm not capable of killing?"

He was. Instinctively Erin knew that without a doubt. A shiver raced through her, a dark and dangerous thrill. "I think you're probably capable of just about anything," she acknowledged.

"That's reason enough to run, isn't it?"

"I'm through running," Erin said, her voice trembling yet angry.

"Then God help you." He lifted a battered hand and brushed the knuckles down her face. It was a soft touch, excruciatingly fleeting. Erin caught his hand when he would have moved away, and her lips skimmed his scarred flesh.

Slade jerked his hand back. "Don't," he said, his

voice cold. "Don't play with fire unless you want to get burned."

He gazed down at her, and the power of the moment frightened Erin. She took one step away from him, but his hand shot out and cupped the back of her neck. He pulled her to him, slowly, deliberately, his shuttered eyes holding her in bondage. She couldn't move away if her life—or her soul—depended on it. His mouth looked savage and predatory as he moved his lips downward, to hers.

"Too late," he whispered, when she made a desperate attempt to escape. "Too late now to run."

Slade's hand tangled in her hair, holding her as he moved in to claim his victory. At first, his lips merely grazed hers with a light, teasing motion, but a bolt of lightning shot through Erin's veins, heating her blood, quickening her pulse. Her heart thundered against her breast.

She was going to swoon, Erin thought, amazed that she even knew such an old-fashioned word, more astonished still that she was going to do it. To have him so close, to have him touching her, kissing her as though she belonged to him. Only him—

Erin hadn't been aware of moving, but suddenly she felt the door behind her back. She was pressed against the wood, and Slade's hands were planted on either side of her head, imprisoning her. His mouth found hers again, and this time the action was neither gentle nor teasing. His tongue stroked hers, coaxing a response she couldn't deny him. He pressed his body against hers, and Erin could feel how hot and hard and ready he was for her. Her senses ignited as she felt her body moving against his.

His hand slid between them and closed over her breast. Erin gasped, frightened by the erotic sensations racing through her. Her hand flew up to grasp his wrist. She tore her mouth from his. "Don't," she said breathlessly.

"What's the matter? The fire getting too hot for you?" His mouth was only an inch from hers. Erin knew he could claim her again whenever he wanted. And she knew she wouldn't be able to resist. Her hand trembled on his wrist.

"It's too soon," she protested.

"You're wrong. It's almost too late," he warned, his voice husky. "In another minute—"

Erin's heart was pounding so loudly she thought for a moment he'd heard it. He was pulling away from her, however, and dimly she became aware of another noise. The telephone was ringing.

A change came over him swiftly. He straightened, looking at once dark and dangerous and in control. He looked as if the past few moments hadn't occurred at all. "I left this number with the station," he said. "It's probably for me."

Erin's heart was still beating against her breast. Butterflies danced in her stomach, and her lips felt bruised and swollen and aching for more of his kisses.

Shaken by the sensations, she watched as he strode across the room and jerked up the receiver. He listened for a minute or two, his expression growing even darker, and when he hung up the phone, Erin knew something else had happened. Something bad.

"What is it?"

"Maybe now you'll listen to reason," he said slowly, walking toward her. "Maybe now you'll leave."

"What's happened?" she asked. The lingering excitement in her stomach turned to fear.

He gazed at her, his emotions hidden. "There's been another killing."

# CHAPTER NINE

$S$lade took Erin with him. There was no way he was going to leave her behind again. Not until daylight, at least. He parked on Fifth Avenue near two patrol cars with flashing lights, and together he and Erin got out. Without a word, they walked through the Washington Arch, toward the group of people huddled near the center of the square.

He glanced down at Erin. What was she thinking? he wondered. What was this doing to her after what she had been through?

Suddenly he wanted more than anything to reach out to her, to draw her into his arms and protect her against the darkness out there, the evil that had touched her life. But how could he? He was a part of that evil, and no matter how many books she wrote, Erin could never really understand what it was like to live in complete darkness, the way Slade had to live.

As if sensing his despair, she touched his sleeve, and he looked down at the smooth, unmarred flesh of her hand. Her face was pale, her eyes frightened. "Nick, I don't think—"

He nodded in understanding. "Wait here," he said,

then strode through the darkness toward the crime scene. The crowd of officers parted as he approached.

Slade stared down at the body for a moment, the feeling of dread tightening like a noose around his neck. He knew her. He knew the victim. He'd seen her at the club. He'd warned her away, just as he had the others.

Outwardly impassive, Slade knelt and tilted the young woman's head. Two trickles of blood ran down her neck and back into her hair. Her eyes were closed, but he remembered how they had looked in life, and he knew how they would look if she opened them again in death. He would have to get her to the morgue as quickly as possible. He would have to see to it that she couldn't come back.

Slade lifted his head, listening to the night, to the wind rustling through the trees. The breeze, he thought. The breeze felt the way it had the night Megan Ramsey had died.

And the night Simone had died.

From a distance, Erin watched Nick as he knelt and examined the body. A shudder ripped through her as she remembered another night, another body. Megan, she silently implored, help us find him. Help us stop him.

Overhead the wind stirred in the trees, and Erin shivered. It sounded like whispers, she thought. Like the moans of despair from a thousand restless souls.

She remembered when she and Megan were little

how their mother had told them about the bodies buried beneath Washington Square. "Thousands," Desiree had said, "waiting to come up and grab little girls like you who don't listen to their mothers."

Even the simple, childish pleasure of playing outdoors had been taken from her because whenever Erin had entered Washington Square, all she could think about were the thousands of bodies upon whose graves she trod. She could feel those invisible eyes watching her, waiting for her to disobey her mother. She could almost feel their arms reaching up through the earth to grab her and take her back down with them.

*We've been waiting for you, Erin.*

Erin shivered at the voice inside her head. Eyes were watching her now, she thought. Hands were reaching for her, but the darkness hid them. The darkness hid all things that didn't want to be seen, didn't want to be revealed.

Mist twisted and coiled in the wind, giving the whole scene a strange movement. Erin's legs grew unstable and she swayed, as light-headed as if she were standing on the prow of a ship. She reached out for support, but found nothing but air.

*Erin.*

At first Erin thought Nick was calling to her, and she felt an enormous wave of relief flood over her. But through the darkness, she saw that he remained near the body as the officer nearest him continued to talk to him. She'd only imagined someone had called her. The wind was playing tricks on her—

*Errinn!*

Erin whipped around, searching the night. There it was again, that plaintive call that clawed at her heart. "Megan." She whispered the name out loud, but the wind tore away the sound. It was so cold out here, so silent. Erin could almost hear the sound of her heart thumping. Wasn't it her own heart she heard?

The rhythmic beating echoed off the wall of mist, so loud now that Erin had to cover her ears with her hands. A thousand hearts pounded beneath her, clamoring for her to come to them, to join their dark ranks. Over and over again they chanted her name. *Erin. Erin. Erin.*

She lowered her hands from her ears and whispered again, "Megan? Where are you?"

*I'm here, Erin. Don't leave me. Don't ever leave me again.*

The voice was real this time. No longer inside her head, it swept down through the trees and penetrated Erin's soul. Erin turned, searching the darkness. "Where?"

*This way.*

As if in a daze, Erin started walking toward the street, toward a shadowy courtyard at the side of a redbrick building. A movement in the enclosure caught her eye. A figure stood at the fringes of the darkness, tantalizing Erin with hardly more than a glimpse. "Megan?"

"We've been waiting for you, Erin." Another voice this time. A dark, male voice, liquid with seduction.

A dangerous languor slipped over her. Erin tried to fight it, tried to resist, but she knew deep inside she couldn't. She'd known all along. Try as she might to ward off the monsters, she'd always known that it was only a matter of time before they would come for her.

Before she would join them.

*You belong to us, Erin. You've always belonged to us. Come. Your sister is waiting for you.*

Erin took another step toward that voice. For just a moment, a cloud blocked the moon, casting the earth in complete blackness. Then it moved away, and moonlight spilled across the square, silvering the mist with a soft, sterling glow. Closer and closer Erin drew toward that place of shadows, to the darkness that lay beyond…and to that beckoning figure that spoke to her soul.

"Erin, no!"

"Let me go!" She tried to shake away the hand that held her arm, but the grip tightened. She looked up into Slade's hidden gaze. "Didn't you hear her?" she asked desperately. "Didn't you hear her calling to me?"

"Hear who?" Slade's fingers dug into her arm

when she didn't answer. "Hear who, Erin? Answer me, damn it! What's the matter with you?"

"I don't know." Her head was clearing now. She lifted a shaking hand to her temple. "I feel so... strange...so weak."

He was holding both her arms, gripping her so tightly that panic bubbled to life inside her. "Tell me what you heard," he demanded in a voice that made shivers run up and down her spine. "Tell me exactly what you heard."

*Tell him nothing!*

And at that moment, Erin understood exactly why she couldn't tell him. Why she couldn't leave New York. Her sister was here, no matter what Nick said. And together they—she and Megan—would find Megan's killer.

Erin was quiet on the way home, and strangely calm. Slade cast her a worried glance. What was she thinking? What was she feeling? She seemed so...different.

As if reading his thoughts, Erin turned and met his gaze. She was smiling a little half smile that made his blood run cold. She didn't look like Erin at all. She looked like Megan. Like Simone.

"What happened back there?" he asked suddenly into the silence. "What did you see?"

"Nothing."

"You said you heard Megan calling to you."

"Megan's dead," she said. There was nothing in her voice that gave away her emotion—no hint of grief, just that awful calm, that terrible acceptance.

"Erin—"

"Don't worry about me, Nick. I'll be fine. I know what to do now."

"What do you mean?"

She smiled again. "You've told me often enough. I'll keep my windows and doors locked. I won't invite anyone inside."

She said the right words, but Slade still felt chilled. "No one," he reiterated. "That's crucial, Erin."

"Yes, I realize that now."

Where was the fear he'd witnessed earlier? The panic he'd seen in her eyes? With something of a shock, Slade realized that she was actually humming softly to herself, a little singsong tune that seemed hauntingly familiar. What had happened back there? he asked himself desperately. What the hell had happened?

He pulled up in front of her apartment and walked her to the door. He went in with her, searching the apartment as he always did before he left. "It's almost dawn," he said. "You'll be safe now."

"Yes," she agreed, "I'll be safe."

But there was something in her eyes....

Slade hated to leave her. He felt an almost overwhelming compulsion to draw her into his arms and hold her tightly, until the sun was shining all around them. But he couldn't do that. He couldn't face the sunlight, even for Erin.

He bent suddenly, urgently, and brushed his lips against hers. She clung to him only for a moment, but her response was oddly reassuring. She trailed her fingertips across his cheeks, skirting the bottom of his glasses. "Don't worry, Nick," she said again. "I know what to do."

That's what worries me, he thought grimly.

"I've got to tell her."

"You know you can't. It would be disastrous."

Slade glared down at Delaney from across the commissioner's desk. It was dawn outside, and Slade had to get home before the sun came out full force. His eyes couldn't withstand the light, not for any length of time. He was cutting it close, coming here this late, but he'd had no choice. He'd stayed outside Erin's apartment until just a few minutes ago because he didn't dare leave her alone, especially not after the strange way she was acting. At least now he knew she would be safe—for twelve more hours. Until sunset.

His temper exploded when he thought about the danger she was in. And it was all because of him. Because he couldn't be honest with her. "Damn it, I've got to tell her." He slammed his fist against the commissioner's desk. "How else can I make her realize the danger she's in? She already suspects, anyway. She couldn't write the books she writes if she didn't already believe, whether she knows it or not.''

"Nick," the commissioner began in a calm, rational voice. Tall, lean, impeccably dressed, Thomas Delaney could be infuriatingly rational. He leaned back in his chair and eyed Slade speculatively. "Let's not lose sight of our objective here. Don't forget the oath we all took. We can't reveal the Mission or its purpose to anyone. If the citizens out there found out what we're dealing with, there would be mass hysteria. Civilization as we know it could crumble, and we would have no way to prevent it. You can't tell her, Nick. You can't tell anyone.''

"Then how the hell am I supposed to protect her? She won't leave until her sister's killer is caught, and I can't be sure she won't be his next target.''

"She hasn't gone to that club yet," the commissioner observed. "That place seems to be the link with the other victims. Except for the old man, of course. And from what you told me, he was the girl's kill.''

"Aren't you forgetting something?" Slade asked darkly. "There's another link. Another reason why those girls were killed.''

"Meaning you."

"Meaning me. And that's all the more reason why I need to be honest with Erin. Believe me, she can handle it.''

"We can't take that chance and you know it. Especially not with someone like her. She already has notoriety because of her books. If she went public with this, it could be the end of the Mission. The end of everything we've worked so hard to accomplish. We'd all be declared insane. Or worse,'' he said dryly.

"There are other things to consider here,'' Slade said angrily. "We're talking about Erin Ramsey's life.''

"I'm counting on you to keep her safe.''

"Like I did Simone?''

A flicker of pain crossed the commissioner's stoic expression. "That wasn't your fault,'' he said softly.

"But Simone is still dead,'' Slade said bitterly. "Because I couldn't protect her.''

What if he couldn't protect Erin? What if he lost her to the darkness, too? He'd already lost *his* soul. How could he survive knowing that she had lost hers, too?

# CHAPTER TEN

$E$rin slept until nearly four o'clock the next day, but her rest was plagued with dreams about her sister. In the dream, she and Megan were walking together in some sort of dimly lit tunnel when suddenly the path split into two different trails. One way held complete darkness. But rather than being frightening, the blackness exuded a kind of mystical excitement, a subtle beauty only visible to the discerning eye.

At the end of the other path, a white light shimmered with radiance. It, too, held a special allure, and for the longest moment, both Megan and Erin stood looking down the two tunnels.

Then suddenly Megan was gone, and Erin had no idea which way she'd gone. ''Megan! Where are you?''

''Here.''

''Which way?''

''You have to choose for yourself.''

And then, when Erin was just about to enter the tunnel with the light, a voice spoke to her from the darkness. A silky, seductive voice, which touched the forbidden desires deep within her.

''This way, Erin. We've been waiting for you.''

''I'm not one of you,'' she whispered.

"You just haven't admitted it yet. But you know, Erin. You've always known that you belong to the darkness."

The dreams went on and on like that until Erin finally shook off the remnants of sleep and got out of bed. But there was something about the voice in her dream, the voice in the darkness, that lingered in her mind. She stared at her reflection in the mirror, hardly recognizing the woman who stared back at her.

*You know. You've always known that you belong to the darkness.*

The voice was right. She had always known. It wasn't the darkness that had always frightened her. It was knowing that she was a part of it that scared her desperately and made her deny what she knew in her heart to be true. You know what you have to do, she said to her reflection.

Blue eyes—Megan's eyes—stared back at her. Then the illusion dissolved as the telephone on the nightstand shattered the silence of the apartment.

Erin crossed the room and picked up the receiver. The voice on the other end sounded oddly familiar to her. Hypnotic, persuasive. "Miss Ramsey? This is Roman Gerard. I'd like to talk to you about your sister, if you have some free time today."

Erin's heart leapt with excitement. "Of course," she said eagerly. "I've been wanting to talk to you, as well. Just tell me when and where to meet you."

"Come to the Alucard as soon as you possibly can. I'm very much looking forward to meeting you."

Erin hung up the phone and hurriedly dressed. This was the break she'd been waiting for. Briefly she thought that perhaps she should call Nick, but almost immediately discarded the idea. He would only try to talk her out of going, and Erin desperately wanted to meet with Gerard, to find out what he could tell her about Megan.

It wasn't until she was almost at the theater that she stopped to consider how in the world Gerard had known about her in the first place, and how he'd known where to find her.

Following the side street that ran parallel to the theater, Erin once again located the stage door. She knocked loudly a few times before the door opened inward, and a shadow appeared in the doorway.

Erin's hand fluttered to her throat as she studied the dour little man standing there. He wore faded overalls and a ragged flannel shirt, and in one scarred hand he carried a bucket. Surely this couldn't be Roman Gerard. "What do you want?" he barked in annoyance. "Theater's closed right now."

"I know. I'm looking for Mr. Gerard."

"Come about the part, have you?" He eyed her up and down with beady black eyes. "You've the right look, I guess. Same as the others. Come back later," he advised.

"Are you Mr. Gerard?"

He cackled like a raven, displaying uneven rows of sharp, dingy teeth. "I'm the janitor, missy. But I reckon I've seen enough of your kind to be able to size you up pretty quick."

"I'm not an actress," Erin said coolly, unnerved by the little man's avid stare. "I've got an appointment with Mr. Gerard. He wanted to see me."

Something changed in his attitude. A cloud drifted over his expression. He cast a quick, uneasy glance over his shoulder. "He ain't here now," he said with a note of urgency in his voice.

"But I thought—"

Something moved in the darkness behind him. Erin had just the briefest glimpse of a tall, gaunt shadow staring at her from the gloom. Then she heard a voice, a beautiful, baritone voice asking, "Who is it, Griffin?" There was a shuffling sound, a low murmur as Griffin turned and spoke into the darkness. Then the other voice said, "Ask her to come in."

Griffin looked as if he was about to protest, then with a dark glare at Erin, he opened the door wider and let her step through.

Inside, the theater was gloomy. The overhead lights in the auditorium, as well as the stage lights, were off, and the electric bulbs in the wall sconces flickered like candlelight, creating an eerie ambience that would immediately draw the audience into the dark atmosphere of the play.

Erin shivered as she gazed around the empty theater. The usual hustle and bustle before the premiere of a show was absent from the Alucard Theater. It seemed deserted, and Erin wondered if the play might have been canceled because of Megan.

Griffin scowled at her from the shadows. "This way," he barked. He led her through a corridor to the right of the stage and up a flight of stairs to a balcony that hung over the auditorium, providing an excellent view of the stage. It was even darker in the balcony, and Erin began to feel scared. Where was everyone?

"Where is Mr. Gerard?" she asked, turning to face Griffin, but the creepy little man was nowhere in sight. Erin looked around for a minute, unsure what to do. Her first instinct was to run as fast and as far away from the Alucard Theater as she could, but in the gloom where she stood, she wasn't even sure she could locate the stairway Griffin had led her up.

Okay, she thought, taking a deep breath. No need to be frightened. This was a theater, after all. There were bound to be rehearsals later. The actresses and actors would all start streaming in any minute now to get into makeup and wardrobe, and without a doubt, the people who worked behind the scenes were already here, making sure props and costumes were all in place. The feeling of aloneness was just her imagination.

But…was it merely a fancy or had the balcony suddenly gotten colder? An icy breeze licked down the

collar of her coat, and Erin tugged it more tightly
around her. She started to ease through the darkness
in the direction she thought the stairs were located,
but suddenly the stage lights came on, illuminating
the area just enough to reveal an elaborately decorated
bedroom.

A woman sat in front of a mirror, brushing her hair,
and though the stage was a long way from Erin and
only dimly lit, she could have sworn that the woman
cast no reflection in the mirror.

Just an illusion, Erin thought. Just a stage prop.

But her legs were trembling in spite of herself.
There was something so very disturbing about the
way the woman looked, the way she was dressed.
Erin couldn't take her eyes off her. She seemed
so…familiar.

And then, as the woman turned and Erin caught a
glimpse of her profile, she knew. The woman reminded her of Megan, enough so that the hair at
Erin's neck prickled. She almost started to call down
to the woman, but caught herself, realizing that it was
all a deception. The woman on stage couldn't be Megan. Megan was dead. Buried. Just a memory, Erin
thought sadly as she watched the stage.

The actress wore a flowing white gown that seemed
hardly more than a whisper of silk, and her long, dark
hair gleamed in the candlelight. As she stroked her
glossy curls, a breeze from the open window drifted
in, and the candle flame danced wildly.

The woman stood, the silhouette of her body through the gossamer gown revealed as she turned toward the window, a look of quiet exultation on her features.

A shadow passed across the window, and then in yet another clever chimera, a man was standing before her. He was tall, extraordinarily thin, but handsome and alluring with an almost regal bearing. He wore dark clothes and his long black hair was pulled straight back, highlighting aristocratic cheekbones and full, sensuous lips.

He took the woman's hand and lifted it to his lips, and the woman looked as if she might swoon. Erin could have sworn she felt his cool, moist breath against her own fingers as she watched the scene unfolding on stage. She lifted her hand to her face and felt the chill of her flesh. Her heart pounded, and for a moment she wondered if she was dreaming. The play was affecting her strangely, as if she had witnessed this scene before. As if she were somehow a part of it.

The man spoke and his voice sent deep chills down Erin's spine. "Such a lovely white neck. Such smooth and tender flesh. Your neck was made for my lips. One kiss, my love. One last kiss before dying."

Erin gasped, recognizing the words from Megan's script. That was why it all seemed so familiar to her. She had read Gerard's *Dark Obsession.* The woman on stage was playing Megan's role. That was why she reminded Erin so much of her sister.

The woman laughed, and the sound echoed eerily in the theater. The man took her in his arms and kissed her. Erin watched as the woman went limp, overcome with passion, and Erin felt her own blood stirring. The man broke the kiss, and bent her backward over his arm so he could trail his lips along her smooth, graceful neck. The woman sighed and whispered her desires.

The lights on stage dimmed even more, and suddenly the woman was alone again. Slowly she lifted her head and gazed straight through the darkness until Erin could have sworn she was staring right at her.

She *does* look like Megan, Erin thought briefly, just before the woman smiled, revealing long, gleaming fangs in the candlelight. Horrified by the scene, Erin ran. Oblivious of the darkness, she fled, almost falling headlong down the stairs before she managed to gain her balance. With one hand she felt along the wall until she was sure she was in the corridor Griffin had led her through. At last she came out of the darkness into the auditorium and located the stage door.

She wanted to hurry, wanted to get out into the last remnants of sunshine as fast as she could, but there was a man standing in a passageway near the door watching her. The intensity of his gaze paralyzed her for a moment, then Erin reached for the knob.

"I wanted to talk to you about your sister." The

beautiful baritone voice, the voice she'd heard on stage, spoke to her from the shadows. Erin's heart pounded like an erratic drumbeat as she felt her hand tremble on the doorknob.

He moved toward her, keeping to the shadows of the passageway. His presence seemed hardly to disturb the darkness surrounding him. There was something familiar about him, Erin thought. Something frightening...

She swallowed, letting her hand fall from the brass doorknob. "What about her?"

"You look exactly like her, you know. She was very beautiful, so vital and...alive, if you know what I mean."

Erin met Gerard's eyes. Again she had a disconcerting feeling that she had seen those eyes before. "Have we met?" she asked suddenly.

Gerard's smile deepened. "It does seem so, doesn't it?"

"How well did you know my sister?" Erin asked abruptly.

He was studying her carefully, his gaze raking over her until Erin grew uncomfortable. She tried to look away from his eyes, but found she couldn't. They were such an odd color. So light they almost seemed to glow in the dim light.

"Megan and I became...quite close. She had a rare talent. She captured the essence of my heroine so…magnificently,'' he added with a strange glint in his eyes.

"I see you've already recast," Erin said. "The actress I saw earlier was very good. In fact, she looks like my sister, too. Uncannily so.''

"Do you really think so?'' Gerard asked smoothly as he moved closer. "The actress is adequate for the role, but she brings no special understanding to it. But you… I have a feeling *you* could capture the spirit of my heroine even better than your sister. Have you any acting experience, Erin?''

She gave a nervous little laugh. "Hardly. I'm a writer.''

"Ah, yes. *Demon Lover.* We have much in common, you and I.''

"Because we both write about vampires,'' Erin said, growing more and more uneasy. The shadows on the wall of the theater loomed, closing in on her.

"Because of so much more than that,'' he said. "Tell me why you felt it necessary to destroy the vampire in the end, Erin. I was very disappointed.''

"He was evil,'' Erin said. "He had to be destroyed.''

"He was only evil to those who could not understand him. Just think of the knowledge he had accumulated over the centuries. The secrets of the universe he had learned, the power he held in the palm of his hand. You destroyed the wrong man, Erin. The heroine should have destroyed the vampire's tormentors.''

"But you did that," she said, "in *Dark Obsession*. Your vampire is the victor.''

"As it should be. Survival of the fittest, Erin.''

Their voices echoed in the empty auditorium, reminding Erin once again how deserted the place was, how abandoned she suddenly felt. "I wonder if we could resume this conversation another time,'' she asked nervously. "I really must go now, but I would like to talk to you more about Megan. Could I come by in the morning?'' When the sun is shining, she thought. When there are people about.

"I'm afraid I'm not a very early riser,'' he said with regret. "Not many of us in the theater are. I often don't arise until most people are sleeping. But by all means, do come back. I feel we have so much in common. I'm eager to talk with you again. Who knows? I might even convince you to resurrect the demon lover in your next book.''

"He's dead,'' Erin said.

"Is he? You never know about a vampire, Erin.''

Erin's hand tightened on the doorknob. She could feel his eyes on her, and for some reason she had the chilling notion that he was looking at her neck.

"Au revoir, Erin.''

Au revoir, she thought as she opened the door and hurried through. *Till we meet again.*

The words made her shiver, made her want to hasten home and bolt all the doors and windows and hide herself away in the apartment until it was morning and she was certain all the monsters had gone away again.

You're being silly, she scolded herself. It's just a play and Roman Gerard is just a man. A very strange man, but just a man. But it was more than that, and Erin knew it. Somewhere inside that theater, somewhere buried in the lines of that play might very well be a clue to Megan's murderer.

In the falling twilight, the theater seemed to wear a pall of gloom. The shadows around her deepened, and the wind grew brisker. Shivering from cold and from a growing uneasiness about Roman Gerard and his play, Erin gathered her coat around her and ran toward the street, anxious to become a part of the crowd of people hurrying home from work.

Just as she reached Washington Square, a mist descended, seeping through her wool coat to chill her to the bone. She tried to shake the lingering gloom, but as she crossed through the square, her past rose up to confront her yet again.

Like a relentless echo, Desiree's voice resounded in her ears. "Did you know there are bodies buried beneath Washington Square, Erin? Thousands, just waiting to reach up and grab little girls like you who don't do as they're told." Back then, she would grab hold of Erin's hand, and Erin would scream and scream while Desiree laughed and laughed.

Beneath the street noises, Erin became aware of a more subtle sound. She heard children's voices repeating the same singsong rhyme over and over again. Her heart froze. She knew that song. It was part of her past. Hers and Megan's.

Erin put her hands to her ears, trying to block the sound, but the singing grew louder until she could no longer deny the words.

Now I lay me down to sleep,
I pray the Lord my soul to keep.
If I should die before I wake,
I pray the Lord my soul to take.

It was the prayer she and Megan had repeated endlessly while they clung to each other during the long, terrifying nights. And as Erin listened more closely, she heard another voice, an achingly familiar voice, rising over the chanting.

*Don't leave me, sissy. Don't ever leave me again.*

"Megan!" She cried her sister's name into the twilight. Immediately the wind picked up, rustling through the trees like a whisper. Like a warning.

Shivering against the cold, Erin hurried toward home. Racine was standing in the hallway when Erin entered the building. "I've been waiting and waiting for you," she said.

"Why?"

Racine's green eyes glittered with worry. "Because

I have to tell you something. We'd better go inside," she said, nodding toward Erin's door.

Apprehension crept up Erin's spine. "What is it?" she asked. "Has something happened?"

Her first thought was that something had happened to Nick. Fear stabbed through her. "Is it about Detective Slade?"

Racine gave her a sidelong glance. "Yes."

"What happened? Is he hurt?"

"Not that I know of." Racine took the key from Erin's shaking hands and opened the door. She turned on the light, then closed the door behind Erin. "Why are you so worried about Detective Slade?" Racine asked suspiciously.

"Because he's working on Megan's case."

"Are you sure that's the only reason?"

Erin walked over to the window and stared out. "What other reason could there be?"

"You're not in love with him, are you?"

Erin whirled to face Racine. "Of course not. How could I be? I barely know him."

"I'm glad you realize that fact," Racine said ominously. "Because you *don't* know him, Erin. You don't know anything about that man."

"What are you trying to tell me?"

Racine walked slowly toward Erin, her expression grave. "I know why he looks so familiar to me," she said. "Why I didn't trust him the moment you introduced him to me." She clutched Erin's hand. "You remember the club I told you about the night Megan was killed? The one down by the river? I saw Detective Slade there one night. I saw him talking to Megan. He knew her, Erin. He knew your sister. And now she's dead.''

# CHAPTER ELEVEN

"Are you sure this is the right place, lady?"

In the dim light from the street, Erin checked the address on the card she held in her hand. This was the place all right.

Her heart quickened as she gazed out at the bleak, ominous-looking club. With its boarded windows and peeling paint, the building would have looked abandoned, save for the small group of people milling about outside, gazing curiously at her cab.

"Well? You getting out or what?"

Erin took a deep breath and fumbled with the door handle. "I'm getting out."

"You gotta be nuts, lady," he muttered, accepting the bills she thrust at him.

"Probably," she agreed, stepping onto the street. With an odd sense of abandonment, she watched as the cab roared away. Then she turned toward the club. Mist curled like smoke around her feet, and a stiff breeze tugged at her coat. Shadows loomed in the shifting lights from the street.

*We've been waiting for you, Erin.*

"You won't get me," she whispered to the darkness. "This time, *I'm* coming for *you*."

Inside, Nosferatu's was crowded, smoky and dark.

Tables were placed inside small curtained alcoves, giving the illusion of privacy, while dark, decadent-sounding music blasted from overhead speakers. Most of the patrons were young, thin and dressed completely in black. And every single one of them wore sunglasses. Their faces all seemed like masks, all so much alike without the eyes to express their emotions.

And Megan had come here. Megan had been obsessed with this place. Megan had talked to Nick here.

What did it all mean? Erin wondered desperately. Why hadn't he told her? Why hadn't he confided in her that he knew her sister?

*Because he has something to hide, that's why.*

Erin closed her eyes as Racine's accusation rang in her ears. "You can't think he has anything to do with the killings. He's a policeman, for God's sake," Erin had protested, not quite knowing why she felt such an overwhelming need to defend him.

"So what? You think the police can't be corrupt? You think a policeman can't become a cold-blooded killer? Who knows what may have driven him over the edge? I'll bet you anything that Detective Slade is a man with a very dark past. I advise you to stay away from him, Erin. He's dangerous. You only have to look at him to know that."

Yes. He *was* dangerous. Erin had known that all along. Then what was she doing here? she asked herself helplessly.

Her heart began to pound even harder in dread and

fear as she gazed around the club. But her heart also raced with a strange mixture of excitement and anticipation. She slipped on a pair of Megan's dark glasses and a feeling of anonymity overwhelmed her.

The deep, pounding rhythm of the music drew her toward the dance floor, where she stood watching. No strobe lights here. No mirrored balls. These people danced in darkness, their movements suggestive, bordering on the erotic, and Erin felt her stomach quiver with nervous tension.

She'd chosen a black knit dress from Megan's wardrobe, and now she blended with the dark atmosphere of the club. She even almost felt a part of it. Don't, she warned herself. Don't let the darkness seduce you. Don't let it trick you.

She hitched herself up onto a metal stool at the bar. The bartender, a tall, gaunt-looking young man with long straggly hair and tiny wire-rimmed sunglasses, approached her.

"Haven't seen you in here before," he said after she'd placed her order. He studied her face in the shadowy light.

Erin smiled nervously as she adjusted her glasses. "How can you tell?"

"Some people study eyes. I study teeth. And I know I've never seen yours before."

His gaze lingered on her lips for so long that Erin began to grow even more unsettled. She took a sip of the wine he placed in front of her and gazed around the club. "Actually, my sister used to come here. Her name was Megan Ramsey."

"I see the resemblance."

He was still looking at her mouth, Erin noticed. She started to moisten her lips, then thought better of the action. Instead she said, "So you remember her?"

"She came in a few times." He leaned his forearms against the bar, and Erin noticed how pale his skin was. Even paler than hers. So pale it almost appeared translucent in the dim light from the bar. "I read about what happened to her in the paper. She was a beautiful woman. Great teeth. Just like yours."

Erin fought the urge to place her hand over her mouth. "Did she have friends who came in here with her? Maybe a boyfriend?"

"She used to come in occasionally with some of the other actors from the theater where she worked. They'd drop in after rehearsals to have a few drinks, unwind." Light reflected off his glasses as he cocked his head slightly. "Come to think of it, I do remember seeing her talking to a man once or twice. They seemed to have a thing going, but I haven't seen him in here for a while."

"Was he part of the theater group?"

The bartender shrugged.

"Do you know his name?"

He straightened up from the bar. "Most people don't give out their names in here. Everyone's anonymous. That's why we wear the shades."

"But you knew Megan's name," Erin noted.

"Megan was an actress. She wanted people to remember her."

"So it stands to reason that the man she was with wasn't an actor. Otherwise he would have given out his name, as well."

"Whatever you say."

"What about the other women who were murdered? Did you ever see them in here?"

"Hey, what is this, an inquisition? I've already talked to the police."

"To Detective Slade?" Erin asked sharply.

"Never heard of him," the bartender said, but his attitude had suddenly chilled. He moved down the bar and began mixing what looked like a Bloody Mary for another customer.

Erin turned on the stool, letting her gaze sweep the crowded club. Was he out there somewhere? Was the man who had killed her sister among that anonymous, androgynous crowd, that writhing throng of nameless, faceless bodies that merged and mingled into a darkness that seemed both surreal and dangerously real? And what would she do if she found him? If he found her?

The back of Erin's neck tingled with excitement and fear and another even more disturbing sensation. Someone was watching her again, she thought. But it wasn't just the passing glance of someone curious. Not even the bolder stare of someone interested.

Someone was studying her with such intensity that she felt the depth of his probe all the way to her soul.

Her gaze traveled over the crowd, then rested on one of the alcoves at the back of the room. The curtains had been pulled closed, obscuring whoever sat inside, but for some reason Erin couldn't tear her gaze away. Someone was sitting behind that curtain, calling to her, reaching out to pull her into the darkness.

Or was she imagining that lure?

*We've been waiting for you, Erin.*

The voice slipped inside her, making cold chills run up and down her spine. Erin knew, with every instinct deep inside her, that she should turn and run, leave that dark and dangerous club and never look back. But she couldn't seem to move, couldn't seem to walk. An ominous spell had descended over her, and all she could do was sit there and listen to that voice inside her head, whispering to her secrets she didn't want to hear.

*I know you're afraid of the night, Erin. You're afraid of what you might find in the shadows. But the idea excites you, too, doesn't it? Just like it did her. The darkness intrigues you even as it repels you. You're trapped between two worlds. Between day and night. Dark and light. One day soon, you'll have to choose....*

Erin felt herself reeling, trapped as if on a merry-go-round. The shuttered faces around her spun, one after another, until they all blended into one.

*Dance for me, Erin. Dance for me as she did.*

She had to be dreaming, Erin thought. She had to be in the throes of a powerful nightmare, because when he commanded it, she suddenly found herself floating toward the dance floor, found herself moving to the erotic beat and listening for that voice throbbing inside her.

*That's it. Let the music take you. See how thrilling the night can be?*

The voice seduced her as the beat of the music thrummed through her, coaxing her to respond with an abandon Erin had never known before. Her breath quickened. Her body trembled. Thrill after thrill coursed through her as the words in her head and the music from the speakers flowed into her soul, seducing her with their dark, erotic allusions.

Erin wanted the music never to stop. She wanted to remain in the darkness forever. Wanted the sensations raging inside her to climb higher and higher. Why had she never noticed how beautiful the darkness could be? It reminded her of—

Nick.

As if she'd conjured him up from a nightmare, he stood before her suddenly, looming over her. His shoulders seemed even broader tonight, his expression more grim. Was he the one who had spoken to her? Seduced her? Erin shivered, waiting.

The collar of his leather coat shaded his face, and like everyone else in the place, he wore sunglasses.

He seemed to fit so perfectly in the dark, eerie atmosphere of the club. His face was tense, rigid, as if he was having a hard time controlling his anger. "What are you doing here?"

"I..." *I was looking for you,* she almost said. Erin gazed around the dance floor, at the undulating bodies all around her. The black knit dress she wore had shifted, baring one shoulder, and her dark hair tumbled about both shoulders in wanton disarray. Her face colored in embarrassment. What was she doing? And what must he think of her?

He didn't wait for her to answer. Instead he said, "Let's get the hell out of here." He led her from the dance floor, and a sudden rage filled her. Not her own anger, she dimly realized, but someone else's. Then it was gone, but Erin was shaken by the sensation, and by an almost overwhelming sense of evil.

A young woman with a wild mane of silver hair sidled by, giving Slade an appraising once-over. Erin could have sworn she heard the girl say, "So long, Slade" before he had steered Erin through the entranceway.

The crowd that had mingled outside when Erin first arrived had now dispersed. Clouds scudded across the sky, partially blocking the moon, and the wind that swept down the street carried the chill of rain. The street was silent and dark, with only the quiet swish of tires from the occasional car passing by.

They were completely alone.

Fear erupted inside her as she gazed up at his rigid profile. There was something about him tonight that seemed different. He appeared even darker, more dangerous. More one with the night.

*"You think a policeman can't become a cold-blooded killer? Who knows what may have driven him over the edge?"*

Slade grabbed her arms and pulled her close. "Why did you come here, for God's sake? Why are you dressed like that?" The anger in his voice sent shivers of alarm down Erin's back. With one quick movement, he ripped off her dark glasses and flung them in the gutter.

"I told you before, I dress like this because people think I'm Megan."

"Including you?" His hands tightened on her arms, and he gave her a little shake. "Can't you see what you're doing, Erin? Can't you see what's happening to you? You're becoming obsessed with her. You're *becoming* her. That's why you came here tonight, looking like…"

"Like what?" Erin challenged.

"Like someone you're not."

She tossed back her hair. "You don't know me. You don't know anything about me. I came here because I had to."

"Why?"

"Because I had to see for myself why Megan was so drawn to this place."

''That's the only reason?'' he challenged. The dark, liquid tones of his voice flowed over her, reminding her how very little she knew about him.

''As long as we're asking questions,'' she said, ''I've got one for you. Why haven't you been honest with me? Why didn't you tell me the truth about Megan?''

His hands dropped away from her. ''I don't know what you mean.''

''You know exactly what I mean. You knew her,'' she said, her voice shaking with emotion. ''You knew my sister. You talked to her inside that club on at least one occasion. I have a witness, so don't bother denying it.''

''I wasn't going to,'' he said quietly. ''You're right. I did see Megan there. I talked to her the night she died.''

Erin's hand flew to her mouth. Without thinking, she started backing away from him. Just as he reached out to stop her, she said, ''Don't touch me. Don't you dare touch me. I'll scream.''

''I'm not going to hurt you,'' he lashed out bitterly. ''I would never hurt you.''

''Did you hurt Megan? Did you kill her?''

He shook his head. ''No.'' His voice sounded oddly hurt. Erin's anger faltered for a moment as she watched him.

''Why should I believe you?'' she whispered. ''How can I believe anything you say to me anymore?

You lied to me, Nick. All this time I've tried to learn to trust you, to believe in you, and now I find out that you knew Megan, and you deliberately didn't tell me. Why? If you didn't have anything to hide, why didn't you tell me?''

''Because I knew you'd look at me the way you're looking at me right now.''

Never had Erin seen such raw emotion on anyone's face before. It made her tremble to think of what his eyes would reveal. ''What else are you trying to hide?'' she asked. She reached for his dark glasses, but Slade grabbed her wrist, held her captive while they gazed at each other in anger.

Then slowly the anger began to fade. Erin's heart sped up, and she saw the quickening of his breath, the slight softening of his mouth. Their lips were only inches apart, and Erin could smell the evocative fragrance of his musky cologne mingling with the scent of leather and the darker, headier night scents that seemed so much a part of him.

Her voice was only a trembling whisper when she said, ''Please. I want to see your eyes.''

''You don't know what you're asking,'' he said bitterly.

His head lowered, moving closer, and Erin trembled with fear and anticipation, dread and excitement. She stared at his shuttered eyes, stared at the man who seemed to be the very quintessence of all her nightmares.

Erin had never reacted this way before. The anonymity of the club had emboldened her earlier, but now she felt exposed, vulnerable, torn between her deepest desires and her darkest fears.

"Why did you have to come here?" he demanded raggedly. He lifted his hand, and his fingers combed roughly through her hair. "Why did you have to dress like this? As if you were dressing for *him*."

"I dressed for you," she whispered. "I came here to find you. I had to see you. I had to know if…" His hand slid down her arm, trailing fire, and Erin took a deep, quick breath. "Nick?"

"I would never hurt you, Erin."

He wouldn't, Erin realized with an assurance she didn't quite understand. Even though she couldn't see his eyes, she knew with instincts she'd never used before, just exactly what it was that Nick Slade wanted from her. And what shocked her even more was the fact that she wanted the same thing from him. She wanted him in a way she couldn't begin to understand.

She lifted her lips in silent invitation. In the instant before his mouth crushed hers, Erin heard him groan, a low, deep, growling sound that reminded her of a wounded animal. Then she thought no more as his mouth moved against hers. Without thinking, Erin parted her lips, welcoming him inside. She felt his hesitation for one split second, then suddenly he was in, his tongue exploring, ravaging, conquering her mouth in masterful possession.

Erin's legs trembled, and she clung to him for support. He trapped her body to his, letting her know just how much he did want her. He was lean and hard and tough, and he made her feel utterly feminine. Utterly helpless, and deeply aroused. Erin heard another groan, a softer, more desperate sound this time, and realized that it was coming from her own lips.

The sound seemed to excite Slade even more. He lifted her as easily as if she were a doll and turned her so that she was backed against his car. He pressed against her, moving his hips so provocatively against hers that Erin thought she would die from the feel of it.

"I need you," he said in a deep, desperate voice. "I need to *feel*—"

The urgency in his tone tore at any control Erin might have been struggling with. His lips were forceful and demanding, yes, but there was something else behind his relentless passion. Other emotions that seemed even more desperate, even more dangerous. The longing and the loneliness she sensed deep within him were more powerful, more threatening than the sexual attraction roaring through her like a steam engine.

"Nick..." she whispered, tingling excitement racing through her. She tunneled her fingers in his short hair, trailed the back of her hand down his face. One finger curled around his dark glasses. "Please," she begged softly, "let me."

He stiffened, pulling away from her so abruptly that Erin might have fallen if not for the car behind her. He took several steps back from her, distancing himself as quickly as he could, and disappointment overwhelmed her.

"That was a mistake," he said, gazing down the alleyway. Erin thought she had never seen an expression so bleak, so defeated. "There's no excuse. Not after—" He broke off in self-loathing, lifting his hands to gaze at them in disgust.

How could she have been that stupid? Erin wondered. And irresponsible. She'd practically thrown herself at him, and he...well, he'd made his intentions perfectly clear. He didn't want her. At first maybe, but not now.

Erin turned away, gazing into the night. She felt cold, lonely, and she wanted nothing more than to go home, to shut herself off from the darkness closing in on her once again. How had she ever thought the night exciting and beautiful? It was cruel and frightening and much, much too deceitful.

"I should be going," she murmured, shoving her hands into the pockets of her coat.

He glanced at her then. "I'll take you home."

"I came in a cab, I can leave in a cab," she snapped.

His mouth thinned as he stared down at her.

"Look, I think there's something we need to talk about." He looked tired, she thought, her heart going out to him in spite of herself. How could she still care about him? she asked herself in despair. After everything she'd learned about him, why did she still want him with an almost unbearable longing? "Get in the car, Erin." He opened the car door and in defeat she slipped inside.

How very much she wanted to see his eyes at that moment, to gaze into the very depths of his soul and see... What? What would she see in Nicholas Slade's soul? Darkness, she thought. Darkness and despair and intense loneliness.

A mirror of her own soul, perhaps. An echo of her own bleak emotions that made her want to reach out to him, in spite of the darkness, in spite of her fears. Or maybe even because of them.

He started the engine and they roared through the dark streets toward home. For several minutes they rode in silence, then his voice broke into the stillness like a quiet explosion. "Damn it, Erin, why didn't you tell me you were going there?"

"Maybe I didn't tell you for the same reason you didn't tell me about Megan," she defended. "Maybe we both should be a little more honest with one another from now on."

"What is it you're asking?"

"Were you and Megan—"

His expression hardened and stopped her. "There

was nothing between us. I barely knew her. I'd seen her at that club a few times, and I'd warned her away from the place, just as I did the others.''

''You mean…the other victims?''

''Yes.''

Erin felt as if someone had just punched her very hard in the stomach. The breath left her lungs in a painful swoosh. ''You mean…my God…are you telling me you knew them all? All the dead women?''

He began to speak, his tone expressionless. ''A lot of young women go into that club looking for…God knows what. They have no idea the trouble they can get into. So I warn them to stay away.''

''What kind of trouble?'' Erin asked.

He turned his head and stared at her. ''Your worst nightmare kind of trouble.''

Slade cursed under his breath when he saw her violet eyes widen in terror and the shadow of suspicion cloud them. She didn't believe him, didn't trust him, and who could blame her? He hadn't been honest with her about anything. At that moment, in spite of Delaney's warning to the contrary, Slade had the almost overpowering urge to tell her everything. To tell her how Simone had died and how Megan had died. To tell her that all the deaths had been his fault in one way or another.

He also had the almost overwhelming need to tell her who and what he was, and to let her fear drive her away from him and make her run for safety.

But Slade knew he wouldn't do it. Couldn't do it. Because his desire to keep her in his life was now the greatest compulsion of all.

He saw her take a deep breath, then their gazes met briefly before she looked away again. She gazed out the window. "You accused me of becoming obsessed with Megan's life, and maybe I have. But do you know why, Nick? Do you know why I feel I have to do this one last thing for her? Because I abandoned her. Just like our mother did. I left her here all alone because I couldn't face the nightmares anymore. She begged me not to go, not to leave her, but I did. I left her and I never came back."

"Is that when you moved to L.A.?"

"It was right after I graduated from NYU. I wanted a new start somewhere without the memories. I wanted to put the past behind me, but what I found out was that it didn't matter where I went or how hard I tried to forget. The nightmares were always there. The monsters of my past followed me everywhere. No matter what I did, no matter how many times I destroyed them in my books, they kept coming back. Do you know what it's like to always live in the shadow of your past, Nick?"

Her words cut through the ice he'd built around his resolve. *Do you know what it's like to always live in the shadow of your past?* He gazed at his scarred hands gripping the steering wheel, and for a moment all he could see were the raging flames, that inferno roaring through decaying wood and rotting fabric to claim a life he had once loved more than his own. He didn't need the marks on his hands to remind him of his torment. The scars inside his soul were even deeper, uglier, still raw after all these years.

He pulled the car to the curb in front of Erin's apartment and shut off the engine. He sat staring out the windshield, still seeing the wall of fire that had separated him from Simone, still hearing her screams echo somewhere inside him. He hadn't been able to reach her through the blaze. He hadn't been able to save her, and because of that, the guilt would never go away.

He'd accused Erin of being obsessed, but so was he.

Beside him, Erin spoke softly, her gentle voice a balm to his wounds. "There are so many other unanswered questions in my life. I'll never know what happened to my mother, why she left us, or why she never came back. I think that's the reason I've never been able to put the past to rest. Why I still have nightmares about my childhood. Because I don't understand why it had to happen."

"And you think if you find out what happened to Megan, it'll make her death easier to accept?"

"Yes," she said quietly. "It has to."

"But what if you're wrong? What if you find you can't live with the truth?"

"What could be worse than not knowing?"

"A lot of things," he said grimly. "A lot of things could be worse."

She shrugged. "Maybe. But at least I won't have to wonder anymore."

Slade saw her look up toward the apartment again. He saw her shudder. And he wanted suddenly to pull her into his arms and never let her go. Was it her loneliness, the despair in those violet blue eyes that drew him as no one ever had before? Not even Simone, who had haunted his dreams for years, had made him feel this way. But it was Erin who haunted him now. Erin he wanted now. Erin he needed with an intensity that took his breath away. Erin, whose innocence soothed the savageness of his black soul.

He wanted to touch her again. Wanted to glide his fingers through the radiance of her dark hair, to whisper kisses along her smooth white neck. He wanted to draw her into his arms, cling to her until the fiery images inside his mind were smothered, condemned to nothing more than cold, lifeless ashes.

But he didn't touch her. Didn't dare. Because if he touched her now, he wasn't sure he'd ever be able to let her go.

"When I close my eyes," she whispered, "all I can see is her face and all I can hear is her voice, begging me not to leave her. But I did leave her, and I'll never forgive myself for that."

Erin turned her face away but not before Slade had seen the tears slipping down her cheeks, and without thinking, he *was* touching her, pulling her into his arms, holding her close. His battered hands smoothed her hair as she cried quietly against his chest.

Slade closed his eyes. He had no right to be touching her with hands that had seen so much blood, wreaked such destruction. He had killed the emotions inside himself a long time ago. The Mission had changed him, made him a part of the darkness he sought to destroy.

He had no right to hold a woman like Erin, but he couldn't let her go. Not now. Now when he had found the one person who needed him almost as much as he needed her.

His lips touched Erin's hair as he felt her tremble in his arms. And for the first time in years, he wished he could be something other than what he was.

# CHAPTER TWELVE

Erin sipped hot tea and huddled inside the afghan Nick had dug out of the closet for her. She knew she should lie down and try to get some sleep, but the moment she closed her eyes, the nightmares would be on her again.

Megan's dead, she repeated to herself. She can't come back. Then why do I keep seeing her? Erin asked herself desperately. Why do I keep hearing her?

Because you're crazy, a little voice taunted her. You've always been crazy. Why else would you write those horrible stories?

"What kind of person would be drawn to the thing that frightens her the most?" she whispered.

"Feeling better?"

Erin jumped slightly at the sound of Nick's voice. He'd been so quiet since they'd come back that she had almost forgotten he was there. She tried a smile, but it fell flat. "I'm okay," she said.

But she wasn't okay, and they both knew it. Erin looked away from his too-perceptive stare.

*You're obsessed, Erin,* she told herself.

"You're exhausted," he said. "Why don't you try to get some sleep?"

"I can't."

"You have to rest."

"Why?" she asked, lifting her gaze to his. "Why do you care what I do?"

"Don't you know?" His voice was rough, untamed, but there was something beyond the edges that captured Erin's attention, that made her eyes flood with tears. There was something in his voice that she hadn't heard in a very long time. Maybe ever.

He sat down beside her on the couch, and without thinking, Erin slipped her hand into his. She stared down at their linked fingers, noticing again the strength their union seemed to create.

"I can't stay here tonight, Erin."

"I know. You have work to do."

"That's not why and you know it."

Her hand trembled in his. "What's happening to us, Nick?" she whispered.

His expression darkened even more. "Nothing," he said. "Nothing *can* happen between us. There isn't room in my life for someone like you, Erin. I've... seen things, done things."

"You've killed," she said, sensing the truth.

"When I had to. But there's more. So much more..." His words trailed off in heavy regret. "There's too much darkness in my life. I can't ever be free of it. I can't even see the sunlight anymore."

Her heart pounded against her breast as she gazed up at him, at the dark glasses that seemed so much a part of him now. "Why? Are you saying—"

"I'm saying I belong to the night, Erin, and nothing will ever change that." He stood and paced to the window, staring out. "I should go now."

More than anything, Erin wanted him to stay, but deep inside, she knew he was right. Nothing could happen between them. Not now, not ever. "I'll be all right," she said. "I'll keep the doors and windows locked. And I won't let anyone inside."

But the moment the door closed behind him, Erin knew she had never felt so alone. She crossed the room to the window and watched him stride across the pavement to his car. He opened the door and climbed in, but instead of starting the engine, he merely sat there. For endless minutes he remained until finally Erin realized that he wasn't going anywhere. He was staying there in front of her apartment, guarding her, protecting her. For the first time in years, she could lie down and sleep and know that the nightmares would be held at bay...by him.

He turned his head up toward her window, and for a moment, their gazes clung in the dark. And Erin sensed something stir to life inside her. Something that felt frighteningly like love.

In spite of Slade's vigil, the voice called to her again that night as Erin lay sleeping. The strange whisper wove through the veil of sleep, arousing her with visions of a night she had never known before.

A tentacle of warm air swirled around her, touching her so intimately she shifted restlessly in her sleep.

"No," she moaned, denying the dark seduction.

"Yes..."

The wind moved over her, touching her lips, her neck, her thighs.... "Nick," she murmured.

For just a moment, the seductive wind seemed to howl in rage. Then the voice whispered inside her, *Not him. Never him. You belong to me. I've been waiting for you, Erin.*

"Who are you?" she breathed.

*Don't you know?*

"Yes," she said. "I know."

*Feel me,* came the command. *Open your eyes and see me.*

Her lids fluttered open, and Erin lay in the darkness of her sister's bedroom as that nameless, faceless entity spoke to her very soul. The voice imprisoned her, seduced her, made her want desperately what she had always feared the most.

Boneless, drifting on the wind, Erin rose up and walked into the living room to stand before the French doors. There was a shadow on the balcony, a dark silhouette that made her breath catch. That made her heart pound in terror and a strange, dark excitement.

*Open the door, Erin. Open the door and invite me inside.*

Erin's hand trembled on the knob. Emotions warred

inside her, but she couldn't fight the command that bade her turn the knob, pull back the door, welcome that dark, familiar figure into her home…and into her soul. The metal slipped beneath her fingers. She gripped the knob tighter, turning…

*Yes! Almost there. A little more…*

She turned the knob, and the door blew open with such force that Erin staggered back. The wind rushed inside, tangling her hair, ripping at her nightgown as she stood staring at the man standing in the doorway. For some reason, she couldn't make out his features, but she could see his eyes. They were glowing silver in the darkness.

"Say it," he demanded in triumph. The beauty of his voice flowed over her, seducing her to obey. "Say the words, Erin!"

She moistened her lips. "Please come—"

"Erin!" The sound of another voice stopped her cold. It wasn't a whisper this time, but a voice that called to her through the layers of fog surrounding her mind. Someone pounded on the front door, and the sound became louder, clearer, more urgent as the other voice began slipping away in a whirlwind of fury. "Open the door, Erin! Let me in!"

"Nick?"

She still stood facing the open French doors. The wind raged around her, fast and furious, as the silhouette on the balcony began backing away, fading more deeply into the night. Suddenly Erin was released from the spell. Just as the front door burst open, she collapsed to the floor, half in a daze, shaking with fear.

Slade stood in the doorway, looking for all the world like a demon spawned by the darkness. He strode into the room, his leather coat open, his dark glasses revealing nothing but reflected moonlight. Erin took all this in with only a minimum of awareness. She tried to draw herself up into a ball, tried to hide her partial nakedness from a gaze that was no less penetrating because it was hidden.

Quickly Slade removed his coat, knelt beside her and wrapped it around her shoulders. He stared at the balcony doors. "What happened?"

"I—I don't know." Erin was shaking so hard she could hardly answer him. "I th-thought I s-saw someone on the b-balcony—"

Slade was up and out the open French doors before she could finish the sentence. He came back moments later, shutting and locking the doors behind him. He bent over Erin, gently lifted her to her feet, then guided her toward the couch.

"Tell me what happened," he demanded. "Every last detail."

"I was asleep," Erin said, trying to clear her mind and remember exactly what had just happened to her, "but I could feel this strange breeze in the room with me. It seemed almost…alive. It…touched me," she whispered, looking away. "I know that sounds crazy."

"Did you see anything outside? Anyone?"

There was a note of urgency behind his query. Erin's eyes shot back to him, seeing a face that was at once strange, yet increasingly familiar; frightening, yet oddly comforting. Something stirred inside her. A restlessness she didn't quite understand. She touched a trembling finger to her lips. "I saw a man. He wanted in—"

"He?"

"Roman Gerard," Erin whispered.

"How do you know?" Slade gripped her arm until Erin winced and tried to draw away. He relaxed his hold, but his voice conveyed his tension. "I'm sorry. But think, Erin. How did you know it was Gerard?"

"I recognized his voice," Erin said, her voice steadier. "I met him at the theater, before I went to the club."

"You went there alone?"

"Yes. I had to see him," Erin said, averting her eyes.

Slade swore under his breath. "The doors were open when I came in. This is important, Erin. Did you open them? *Did you invite him inside?*"

"No, but I—" She stopped as she began to remember more and more. The strange wind. The provocative whisper. The dark coercion. She closed her eyes in shame. She had almost invited him in. She hadn't been able to help it. If Nick hadn't come—

She opened her eyes and gazed up at him. "How did you know to come?" she asked. "How could you know that I needed you?"

Because I was afraid, Slade thought. But he said only, "I didn't like the idea of your being here all alone."

"I'm always alone," she said bravely, but he could see that her hands were trembling. Her eyes were soft and blue and very inviting. Almost against his will, Slade's gaze traveled over her. The wide neckline of her cotton nightgown emphasized her creamy shoulders, her sleek neck. Like a subtle invitation, like a promise whispered in the dark, her breasts lifted slightly as she drew a long breath.

Slade closed his eyes tightly. "Get some clothes on," he said hoarsely.

"What?" Her hand flew to her neck, and Slade saw her fingertips caress the spot where the silver cross had once lain. It was dawning on her that its being gone truly did mean that she had no more defenses.

And neither did he, God help them.

"You can't stay here alone tonight," he said flatly, as he got up and moved back to the window. He stared into the night with a brooding frown, seeing in his mind's eye the nameless, faceless shadows wandering the streets, waiting and watching for the unsuspecting. The innocent.

Roman Gerard, he thought. Not D'Angelo. At least now he knew he was dealing with a real entity, and not a ghost from his past conjured up by his guilt.

Behind him he heard Erin stir to life. She got up and crossed the room toward him. He didn't turn around, but he knew she was behind him. He could smell lilacs and sunshine and the essence of innocence that emanated from her like the most seductive perfume. There was an erotic undercurrent to her scent now, as if something dark and powerful had been awakened inside her.

Slowly he turned and gazed down at her. "Get dressed," he said again. "I'll take you to my place for tonight. Gerard can't come to you there. You'll be safe."

But would she be safe from him?

The moment she walked back into the living room, Erin could feel Nick's brooding stare on her. She wore her own clothes this time—jeans and a sedate lavender blouse—but for some reason they didn't seem to suit her anymore. Erin didn't understand why her own clothes felt so foreign to her and Megan's felt so right. She didn't understand all these new feelings whirling around inside her, either. Or why she was drawn to a man who also frightened her.

Slade took the overnight bag from her, and Erin shrugged into her coat. Within minutes they were inside his car, speeding through the darkened streets.

Erin was surprised to find that his apartment was located near the river, not far from the club they'd left earlier.

The area seemed even darker now, and more mysterious than ever. Slade pulled up to the front of a warehouse, activated the garage-door opener, then drove the car inside and lowered the door. Erin shivered as she stepped out of the car into a gloomy, cavernous room. A chill hung in the air as if the mist from the river had seeped through the cracks around the doors and windows. The warehouse reminded her of a tomb. Not that she actually knew what a tomb felt like, she thought, trying to suppress a shudder.

Slade's hand on her elbow made her jump. "Sorry. Not much light down here. Watch your step." But he seemed unaffected by the darkness. He still wore the dark glasses as he guided her deeper into the gloom.

Toward the back of the warehouse, the light completely gave out, and Erin lost all sense of direction. If not for Slade's grip on her arm, she would have been hopelessly lost. As it was, she felt strangely excited.

Slade released her long enough to slide up the wooden panel at the front of a freight elevator. They stepped inside and he flipped the switch. Still in darkness, they began to ascend. Within seconds, the car bounced to a stop, the panel slid up, and they stepped directly into Slade's apartment. "Home sweet home," he murmured, turning on a lamp.

Though not as large as the room downstairs, the apartment still seemed huge, and the same chill pervaded the air. Erin tugged her coat more tightly around her as she walked slowly to the center of the room and looked around.

"I'll try to get some heat going," he said, disappearing into a shadowy hallway. When he returned, he'd taken off his coat. He wore jeans, black boots and one of the dark sweaters he seemed to favor.

Erin's gaze lingered on him for a second too long. When her eyes lifted, she knew that he was staring back at her, and there was something about his expression that suggested he was not unaffected by her perusal.

"How about a drink?" he asked abruptly. "I think I have a bottle of brandy around here somewhere." He moved off toward the kitchen, which occupied a modest corner of the huge room.

"Sounds good." Erin wandered around the living area, fascinated by Slade's home. The furnishings were sparse, consisting mainly of a battered leather sofa and chair, an intricately carved chest that looked like an antique and served as a coffee table, and one wall of crowded bookshelves. "You must read a lot," she commented. It gave her a thrill of pride to see some of her own titles among his books. Erin had never exactly envisioned him as the type who spent long hours glued to a book, especially not foreign editions, as many of these were. "Do you speak all these languages?"

"A word or two here and there."

It took more than a word or two to get through a five-hundred-thousand-word tome, Erin thought. She read through some of the titles. Many of them were books dealing with the supernatural. With vampires.

A chill of foreboding crept over her as she looked back at him. The dark glasses he wore seemed to mock her. "If you don't believe that vampires exist," she said slowly, "why do you have all these books about them?"

"If you don't believe in vampires, why do you write about them?" he countered. He walked slowly across the room and handed her a glass. Erin took the drink and lifted the glass to her lips, craving the fortification. The liquid seared a path all the way down her throat, then raced through her veins. She coughed but almost immediately felt a pleasant little glow chasing away the chill. "That's nice," she said, taking another sip.

Slade reached for her glass. "I wouldn't overdo it if I were you. This stuff can have a kick if you're not careful."

"Are you always so protective?"

He shrugged. "Comes with the job."

"You don't have to stay with me, you know. I can take care of myself."

"So you keep saying. I've yet to see evidence of it, though."

"I'm still alive, aren't I?" she said testily.

"For the time being."

God, he was cold, she thought. Like ice. Did he even have a heart? "Aren't you on duty?" she asked thinly. "Don't you have to get to work?"

"This is work," he said. "Keeping you safe is now my first priority."

"I'm flattered," she said dryly, slipping out of her coat and draping it over the back of the chair. "As long as we're both here for the duration then, we might as well talk about the case. You have to admit all this business about vampires seems to be a bit much for coincidence. You can't tell me you haven't thought the same thing."

"What? That a vampire's on the loose?" His deep voice taunted her.

"You don't have to make it sound so totally insane," she said, an edge in her voice.

She turned back to the bookshelves, skimming over the titles until her gaze lit on a small silver frame tucked into a corner of one of the shelves. Other than the books, it was the only personal adornment she'd seen in the apartment. She picked up the frame and, in the lamplight, studied the couple in the picture.

The young man's arm was draped possessively around the girl's shoulders as she smiled up at him in adoration. Obviously a couple very much in love,

Erin decided. Then she realized with a jolt that the man was Slade, without his dark glasses. She lifted the picture closer, trying to see his eyes, but the photo had been taken from a distance, obscuring his face.

Erin glanced up. "Who is she?"

Slade's face seemed even more shadowed than usual, even less expressive. "Her name was Simone."

Simone. So that was her. Erin studied the girl's long, flowing hair, her lovely, flawless face. She was very beautiful, but there was something disturbing about her....

"You obviously loved each other very much," Erin said. She replaced the frame on the shelf and turned back to Nick.

"That was a long time ago," he said. "In another life."

"What happened?"

He lifted his glass and killed the remainder of the brandy, then said in a toneless voice, "She died."

"I'm sorry." He still clutched the empty glass, and Erin could see the scars that marred the back of his hand. "A fire," she murmured, without thinking.

Slade's gaze sharpened on her. "How did you know about the fire? Who told you?"

"No one. But the scars on your hand...I just assumed..." Her voice trailed off under his scrutiny. "What happened?"

He turned away from her. Erin saw him lift his

hand and remove the dark glasses and rub his eyes wearily. She had the strongest impulse to go to him, to make him turn around so that she could look up and see, for the first time, the emotions that would be revealed in his eyes. She didn't. Instinctively she knew he wasn't ready for that. She wasn't sure she was, either.

He turned again, dark glasses in place. "It doesn't matter anymore."

"But I think it does," she said softly. "I think it matters a great deal. Mr. Rubinoff said you started wearing those glasses after she died. Why?"

"The past is dead. Leave it buried."

"But it isn't, is it?" Erin said sadly. "Yours or mine."

He walked to the window and stood staring out.

Erin came over and stood behind him. "I'd like to know about Simone," she said quietly. "I think I *need* to know."

He remained silent for so long that Erin thought he wasn't going to tell her. Then he said in that dead voice, "It happened eight years ago. Simone and I had just gotten engaged when…she met someone else."

"You must have been very hurt," Erin murmured, not quite knowing what to say.

"Drake D'Angelo fascinated her," Slade said, turning to face Erin, "from the first moment she saw him. She started acting differently, dressing differently. She thought about him day and night. Even when she was with me. Especially when she was with me."

Erin wanted to touch him, connect herself with his pain. But he wouldn't welcome the intimacy, and she knew she didn't have the nerve to push it. So she said simply, "I find that hard to believe."

His smile was bleak. "Do you?" He turned back to the window, staring out at the darkness. "She left me soon after she met him. I was angry and hurt. I went to confront them. There was a struggle. A fire broke out. Simone and Drake were both... destroyed."

Destroyed. What a strange way of putting it, Erin thought. Where moments before the brandy had warmed her, now his words, hanging in the air as heavy as a lingering fog, chilled her to the bone. *"There was a struggle. A fire broke out. Simone and Drake were both ... destroyed."*

He wasn't telling her the truth. Not the whole truth, anyway. What more was he hiding from her? What had really happened that night? Erin wondered with a shudder of unease. Why was the past—an accident—still tormenting him so? Unless...

*"You think a policeman can't become a cold-blooded killer? Who knows what may have driven him over the edge? I'll bet you anything that Detective Slade is a man with a very dark past. I advise you to*

*stay away from him, Erin. He's dangerous. You only have to look at him to know that.''*

"It *was* an accident," she said, almost fiercely, as if to deny her own conclusions. "You shouldn't blame yourself."

"Then who should I blame?" he asked with a harsh edge to his voice. "I failed her. I should have known what to do, but I didn't. I didn't know how to save her. Because of me, she had to die." In spite of her previous resolve, Erin found herself reaching out to touch his arm. He flinched. "Don't," he warned. "Don't get close to me, Erin."

"I'm not Simone," she said.

"And I'm not who you think I am. Don't you understand? People are dying because of me. Women just like you." He grasped her shoulders, holding her at arm's length. "Damn it, stop looking at me that way."

"What way?" Erin's heart pounded inside her chest so loudly she thought she could hear the echo in the icy crypt of a room where they stood.

"Like you want this as much as I do," he groaned, pulling her into his arms so fast Erin stumbled. He caught her, then crushed her to him, tunneling his fingers through her hair to turn her face up for his kiss. "God, it's been so long," he murmured huskily. "So very long since I've held someone like this."

It was a desperate joining. An urgent attempt to wipe out the past. Erin trembled in his arms, telling herself that it didn't matter. It didn't matter that he was trying to forget Simone. She had her own memories to erase. They could use each other. What would be the harm?

"This is wrong," Slade said raggedly, when they finally had to break apart to breathe.

"Because of her?"

"Because of you." His voice gentled as he caressed her face with one scarred hand. "I shouldn't be touching you. Not like this. But I can't help it."

She might have resisted his passion, but not his longing. She might have denied his desire, but not his need. Not the loneliness and despair she sensed inside him, in the soul that mirrored her own. "Then don't," she whispered urgently against his lips, pulling his mouth back to hers. "Don't fight it."

His kisses were like nothing she'd ever known before. He teased her mouth open, then demanded her compliance. His body moved against hers, then commanded her response. Erin wanted to melt in his arms. He was a master of seduction, invading her mouth and her heart and her soul with his shattering kisses.

At last he tore his mouth from hers, pulling her against him to cradle her head against his shoulder. She felt his lips in her hair, then heard him warn, "We have to stop this, Erin. Before it's too late."

"But I don't want to stop," she protested.

"Don't you know what will happen?" he demanded. "If I kiss you one more time, if I hold you even for a minute longer, I won't be able to stop. I'll rip your clothes off right here and now, and I'm not even sure I can manage to be gentle.''

His words made her shiver all over. Made her ache with an arousal that was both wondrous and frightening. ''Maybe I wouldn't want you to be,'' she whispered, amazed by her candor. She took a deep breath, her gaze searching the darkness of his face. ''If we...if we make love, will that satisfy this longing? Will it make the past disappear? Will it be enough, Nick?''

''I don't know.'' His tone was bleak. ''But I do know that I can't offer you anything more. I want you, God knows I need you, but beyond tonight, I can't have you, Erin. I want you to understand that.''

She said ruefully, ''If we do this, you want my eyes wide open, is that it?''

''At least in the beginning.'' She could hear the smile in his voice, and it surprised her. *He* surprised her. Fascinated her. Thrilled her.

She turned and gazed up at him. ''Then perhaps we should both have a clear vision of the future,'' she said softly and reached up to remove his dark glasses. She could tell when he tensed, but he didn't try to stop her this time. Slowly Erin drew the glasses away from his face and stared up at him. Her heart pounded and her pulse quickened. ''My God,'' she breathed. ''Your eyes...''

# CHAPTER THIRTEEN

His eyes. His beautiful, beautiful eyes. So light a shade of gray they appeared almost transparent, like bits of crystal ringed with smoke. They reminded Erin of a rainy night, of a storm brewing at sea.

His eyes. So revealing and all knowing. She could see his desire for her, his need to possess her burning in those crystalline depths, and it made her tremble with her own needs. Made her shiver with fear, because a part of her knew that when it was all over, she would never be the same again.

Her defenses would be gone. She would be alone, but lonely now, no longer content to hide in the shadows of her past. For a moment she glimpsed the bleak years crawling by, years without Nick. Years without love. The thought became almost unbearable.

But his eyes. His eyes made her want to forget all that, made her want to think only of the present and of having him hold her in his arms. His eyes made her quiver with anticipation for the fulfillment the next few moments would bring her. His eyes made her want what she had never had before.

He took her hand in his. Silently they moved to the bedroom and stood in the moonlight, kissing, touching one another, fingers fumbling with clothing as they undressed. Erin's heart thundered in her ears. She couldn't stop looking at his eyes.

"Why do you hide them?" she whispered.

He paused, his gaze holding her in thrall. "They say the eyes are a window to the soul. I've never wanted anyone to see mine."

"Not even me?"

His smile was almost grim. "Especially not you. I didn't think you'd like what you saw." Erin glimpsed a deep sorrow in those gray depths, a dark loneliness that took her breath away, and it gave her a small measure of comfort to know that when he had to leave her, it wouldn't be without regret.

When the last of their clothing dropped to the floor, Slade stared down at her.

"Erin," he said raggedly, "do you have any idea how beautiful you are? How much I want you?" The intensity of his gaze made her tremble. Unconsciously, Erin took a step back, but his arm shot out and he grasped her, imprisoning her as much with his eyes as with his hand. "Do you want to stop this, Erin? It's not too late. Say the word—"

"No," she said fiercely. Her gaze raced over him, and she felt her cheeks flush with heat. He wanted her. There could be no denying that, and a surge of strength flowed through her accompanied by a thrill of excitement. "I don't want to stop. I want this. I want *you*. Oh, Nick." She reached for him and he enfolded her in his arms. Erin closed her eyes, almost overcome with emotion. "I've been dead inside for so long. With you, I feel so—"

"I know." His arms tightened around her as his lips touched her hair. "Believe me, I know." He cupped her face in his hands, tilting her head back as his lips slowly descended toward hers. Erin trembled inside with wanting, with needing him so.

How could a kiss be so passionate and demanding, and yet so tender and giving? Be so possessive, and yet so empowering? Erin had never felt so weak and yet so strong as she did in his embrace. She wrapped her arms around his neck and pulled him close, letting their bodies touch as their tongues entwined, the kiss deepening with an abandon that made her heart race.

He lifted her, bringing their bodies even more intimately together, and Erin gasped, breaking the kiss. She clasped his shoulders, and her head tipped back as his lips moved to her neck, found the pulse point that gave away her excitement, and lingered. Then he bent his head further, and his mouth found her breasts. He caressed each tip with his tongue, and the exquisite sensation he created nearly drove Erin crazy. Her nails dug into his shoulders as she cried out.

Slade answered her passion with a low, desperate groan, fitting their bodies together even more tightly as he moved across the room to the bed, letting her tumble gently backward, still holding on to her. He positioned himself over her, and their lips were only inches apart as she gazed deeply into his eyes.

"I've never felt like this…" She trailed off, unable to voice her emotions.

"Like what? Tell me how you feel, Erin," he demanded, tracing a finger across her lips.

Erin shuddered, her body responding to even so slight a touch from him. "Excited," she replied huskily, glorying in the feel of his body on hers. "Desperate. Frightened."

"You're afraid of me?" The deep, liquid tones had never sounded so gentle.

"You're like the night," she murmured. "You scare me and yet you fascinate me. You make me want to learn all your secrets. You make me want to be…a part of you somehow."

"I want that, too," he said softly, his eyes glowing with an inner fire that warmed Erin all the way to her soul.

"Nick," she whispered, "Please…"

"Yes," he breathed, his lips against hers. "I'll take care of everything, Erin." And then his mouth sought hers once more as he pulled her to him in an embrace so passionate that Erin felt breathless and shivery and utterly protected. Her fears ebbed away as the desire mounted between them.

One kiss melted into the next. One touch led to another. For an eternity, Slade possessed her body with his lips and his hands and his eyes. And when Erin thought she could stand no more, when her body screamed for that final, ultimate release, he joined his body with hers, making her a part of him.

The shock of him inside her made Erin cry out. Instantly Slade's movements stilled. "Did I hurt you?" he asked, his expression shuttered, as if he didn't want her to see the exertion of his control.

"No," Erin said quickly. "It's just…it's been so long…and only a few times…" Her face flamed at the acknowledgment.

Slade buried his face in her neck. His lips grazed her cheek. "It's all right," he whispered. "Do you want me to stop?"

"No." The discomfort was gone now, Erin realized, and in its place was a sense of fulfillment, a feeling of completeness she had never known before. She gave a slight movement with her hips and a thrill of excitement raced through her. "Don't stop," she pleaded, running her fingers through his hair. "I'll die if you stop."

"So will I," he groaned, and his body began to move inside her once again.

He held her as Erin had never been held before. He touched her in a way Erin had hardly dared dream of. He whispered to her, telling her things that made her breathless with excitement, that made her want him even more. If this was darkness, then Erin wanted to be lost in it forever.

A new sensation sprang up inside Erin. With every thrust it grew and strengthened until she wondered how she would be able to stand it. She'd never felt such pleasure, never experienced such closeness with another. It made her want to draw him deeper and deeper inside her. It made her want the night to never end.

But the pleasure turned to frantic urgency. She clutched the sheet with anxious fingers. "Oh, Nick. I don't think...I can do this...."

"Let it happen," he said deeply. He kissed her brows, her nose, her lips. "Let go."

"But I feel so...helpless...."

"Trust me," he murmured. "Just trust me." He quickened his thrusts, responding to the demands of her body. Erin was on fire. She couldn't think, couldn't breathe, could only feel. She looked up into his eyes, his beautiful, beautiful eyes, and felt the world shatter around her.

Slade stared into the darkness, his arms wrapped around Erin as she slept. Lying here like this, she seemed so vulnerable, so light and fragile. Yet he knew she could be strong when she had to be. He'd witnessed her resolve more than once. But would it be enough to sustain her when she found out the truth—about him, about everything?

God, he wished she never had to know. He wished he could hold her like this forever, shutting out the rest of the world, hiding her away from the evil that stalked the night. He wished at that moment for so many things.

If only the guilt he harbored would go away and free him to love a woman like Erin. But that was impossible, as remote a possibility as water on the moon. Slade could never have someone like her. The darkness in his life would taint her. Already he'd stolen something precious from her; he had taken her trust. What more would he wrest from her before all was said and done? Her life? Her soul?

He got up, slipped on his jeans and walked into the living room. He poured himself a glass of brandy, carried it to the window and stared out into the darkness with a brooding frown.

What had he done? he asked himself in disgust. What the hell had he done to Erin tonight? He'd brought them together as closely as a man and woman could be. He'd forged a bond between them that wouldn't be easily severed, no matter how many miles—or how much darkness—separated them. He'd made her need him almost as much as he needed her.

It was strange, he thought grimly. He'd never thought much about loneliness, but already he ached inside at the thought of a time when she would no longer be in his life, when the glimmer of light she'd brought back to him would be taken from him once again.

A noise from the bedroom startled him, and he whipped his head around to listen. It sounded like a groan, and he wondered as he headed toward the door if Erin might be having a nightmare, or if she might be sick. He stood stock-still in the doorway, arrested by the sight that met his eyes.

Erin was lying on top of the covers, moonlight silvering her naked body with a soft, subtle glow. Her dark hair spread like an exotic fan across her pillow as she tossed her head back and forth. She muttered something, and Slade stepped closer, straining to hear. Chills raced up and down his spine.

"No," she moaned. "Please, no."

The bedroom seemed strangely cold. Slade's eyes narrowed as he looked swiftly around the room. The window was cracked slightly, and a draft of wind seeped through. Dead tree limbs scratched against the glass like a lost soul trying to get in.

Slade's gaze went back to Erin as she moaned again and twisted on the tangled sheets, almost as if she was in the throes of deep ecstasy. With a start, he realized that he was getting turned on watching her, even though a part of him felt betrayed. Angry. She was indeed dreaming, and it obviously wasn't a nightmare. Suspicion seeped its way into his mind. Just who the hell was she dreaming about?

The breeze outside picked up, and the feel of it inside the room made Slade's flesh crawl. There was something unnatural about it. Something evil. Something that reminded him of a night eight years ago—

He strode across the room and slammed down the

window. Erin's movements immediately quieted. She lay back against the pillow, sighing softly. In regret or in relief? he wondered.

Slade stalked over to the bed and leaned over her. "Erin, wake up. You were having a dream." He gave her arm a little shake.

Erin's eyes flew open. For a moment she looked dazed, lost, then her eyes cleared and she gasped, jerking the sheet over her naked body and clutching it to her chest. "What happened?" Her eyes were wide with shock, and something else, something that looked a little bit like guilt.

"You tell me," he said. "Just who were you dreaming about?"

A spark of anger flashed in her eyes before she lowered her gaze. "You," she said. "I was dreaming about you."

He tightened his hold on her arm. "Are you sure about that?"

"Yes," she uttered softly.

Take it easy, he told himself firmly, realizing his error. None of this was Erin's fault. He was letting the memories get to him. Just because Simone had dreamed of someone else when he'd held her in his arms didn't mean the same would happen with Erin. Drake D'Angelo was dead, he reminded himself for the umpteenth time. Simone was dead. The past was dead. But he and Erin were alive. Wasn't that all that mattered?

He loosened his grip and rubbed his hands up and down her bare skin. She was so soft and smooth and felt so damned good. He wanted her again, he realized. He wanted her moaning and writhing again, but beneath *him* this time. Or on top of him. He didn't give a damn, just as long as it was him she made love to. So long as he was inside her and soon. Just as long as she knew that she belonged to him—at least for tonight.

He could tell by the subtle glow in her eyes that she wanted him, too. Slade stood and tugged off his jeans, kicking them aside as he stepped toward the bed and climbed in beside Erin. He gathered her in his arms and she turned willingly toward him, lifting her lips for his kiss before he even had time to think.

She was so eager, he thought. Gloriously giving but not without her own demands. In fact, she was quickly taking the lead this time. She shoved him on his back, trailing kisses over his face, down his neck, until her tongue flicked across the pulse in his throat.

He tangled his fingers in her hair, drawing her face up to his for a long, deep kiss. His tongue plunged inside her mouth, and she groaned erotically, stirring his blood even more. He wanted her. All of her. Over and over and over. He didn't think he'd ever get enough of her. Not in this lifetime.

He drew her over him until she was straddling him, and then he pulled her close until he could taste first one breast, and then the other. She gasped, her breath coming in fast little pants as she straightened, tightening her thighs around his hips. She reached down and her hand closed over him. Slade thought he would explode from the sensation. She was so bold, he marveled. Not at all like the Erin of a little while earlier. A wave of uneasiness washed over him, but her hand was moving on him, exerting just the right amount of pressure, and he couldn't think of anything else at the moment.

"Enough," he rasped, propelling himself forward to grab her. He rolled them both over until she was on the bottom and he was lying over her. This time, he was the one who reached downward, parting her thighs with his hand, feeling her moist heat with his fingers. She lifted her hips, inviting a deeper touch and Slade removed his hands, thrusting inside her. He set a fast rhythm and she immediately responded, her untutored movements an aphrodisiac to his already heightened senses. "Who were you dreaming about, Erin?" he gasped, driving inside her deeper, harder, faster, until he thought the whole damned universe must be spinning out of control around them. "Who?" he said again.

"You." Her nails raked across his back as she clung to him, drawing him even closer.

"And who are you making love to?" he demanded.

"You. Only you."

"Say my name. I have to hear you say my name."

''Nick,'' she moaned, and it sounded like a wanton plea.

He felt his control slipping away. He thrust inside her one final time, and she shuddered in his arms as his own release sent him soaring.

Sated, exhausted, Slade felt himself drifting off to sleep a few minutes later, holding Erin in his arms. He roused himself, knowing there was still much to do that night.

Erin nestled herself more firmly against him, and even in his half-asleep state, Slade couldn't help but respond. He trailed a lazy kiss along her cheek, tugging at her lobe with his teeth. ''Who did you just make love with, Erin?'' he asked softly.

''You,'' she murmured drowsily, and then added something that sounded like ''my love.''

It was a long time before Slade could bear to let her go. Finally he slipped out of bed and dressed, then bent to brush his lips against hers. She clung to him, making him wish he could climb back into bed with her.

''I have to go out for a while,'' he said. ''You'll be safe here.''

She was awake now, staring at him with wide, frightened eyes. ''Where are you going?''

''To find Roman Gerard,'' he said, slipping on his dark glasses.

''But what if...what if he's...''

''I know what I'm doing, Erin. Don't worry about

me. You just stay inside here. And don't invite anyone in. Is that clear?''

Yes, she thought. It had always been clear. She just
hadn't wanted to admit what she had always known
was true.

Vampires really did exist.

And Nick knew it, too.

# CHAPTER FOURTEEN

The Alucard Theater slumbered in deep shadow. The black brick facade blended eerily with the night, making it seem almost an illusion in the darkness. Slade tried the front door and found it locked, but when he tried the stage door off the alleyway, the knob turned in his hand and the door swung silently inward.

He slipped inside. The cavernous interior seemed to echo with the thunderous applause from a thousand performances. The curtain was pulled on the stage, shielding what lay beyond, but Slade paid it little attention, anyway. His gaze scanned the auditorium, taking in the rows and rows of sagging seats.

A balcony hung suspended by what seemed no more than imagination over the back half of the theater, and as Slade gazed upward, something stirred in the shadows.

Slowly he climbed the steps to the balcony, remembering everything he'd learned about Roman Gerard in the past few days. An eccentric director who never left the theater. A recluse who never showed himself to anyone. A man who, from all accounts, had a pretty dark secret to hide.

A rat scurried across the floor of the balcony as Slade looked around. He went back down the stairs and searched in the darkness for a door that might lead to a basement or cellar or a room without windows. If Roman Gerard was a vampire, his coffin would be around here somewhere. Unless, of course, he'd had it moved.

Slade located a trapdoor on stage and lifted it to reveal a flight of stairs leading down into complete blackness. Cautiously he descended, playing the flashlight he'd brought with him on the dripping ceiling and walls. Dampness pervaded the air, a kind of seeping cold that put his senses on the alert. Something clung to the moisture, an odor so subtle anyone else would never have noticed it, but Slade recognized it immediately for what it was. Decay. The decline of untold ages. This was a very old passage.

There was no sign of a coffin, but as Slade made his way out of the theater, he experienced an almost overwhelming sense of dread, a premonition that stirred old memories to life and made him remember a past he wanted desperately to forget.

*"Kiss me, Nick. Just one last kiss..."*

The darkness was playing tricks on him, he thought as he left the theater. He knew the voice was coming from within his soul. He knew Simone's plea would never be silenced easily. After all, it hadn't diminished in eight long years. Why should it now?

The breeze outside picked up, and the shadows in the alley deepened. The voice he heard in the wind now was as ageless as the moonlight and as immortal as time itself.

*"You pathetic human,"* it whispered. *"I did nothing to Simone that she didn't want. She and I were meant to be together. I waited centuries for someone like her. You killed her, Slade. You killed her and now I will see you in hell."*

Slade's gaze lifted as something swept across the moon. A chill of foreboding plunged through him. Was it a whisper or the wind he'd heard? Slade knew he was being taunted, but whether by a real enemy or his own demons, he had no idea.

The wind began to howl around him, whipping at his long leather coat like a hound from hell snapping at its leash. When a dark figure emerged from the shadows, Slade's hand closed over the wooden stake he carried.

His breath rushed out in relief as he watched Dr. Traymore walk through the alley toward him. "What the hell are you doing here?"

"The same thing you are, I imagine. Looking for Gerard. He's a vampire, you know."

"How did you find that out?" Slade demanded.

"I have my methods, Detective, the same as you. You and I have a common cause. We just go about it a little differently. We both want to rid the world of vampires. You by killing them, I by curing them."

"Curing them?" Slade scoffed in disgust. "The only cure is a stake through the heart."

"That's effective, but does nothing to save their immortal souls, I'm afraid."

"And your way does?"

"Possibly. Tell me something, Detective. How did someone like you become a vampire hunter?"

"It's a long story."

"It was because of her, wasn't it? Your fiancée, Simone."

Slade stared at him. "How did you know—"

Traymore's smile cut him off. "I know a lot about you, Detective. I've made it a point to study you. I went to the library and read all the accounts about the fire eight years ago, the one that very nearly ended your career. You refused to answer questions. You holed yourself up in an old warehouse down by the river. You started wearing dark glasses to hide your eyes. And you never, ever came out in sunlight. It was easy to draw conclusions."

"And just what conclusions did you draw?" Slade asked bitterly. "I didn't kill Simone."

"Oh, I realize that. Probably better than you do. The conclusions I drew were that the man with her, D'Angelo, was a vampire and that he'd made her one. And I suspect that she tried to turn you, as well. That's why the dark glasses. Your eyes are now sensitive to light, I imagine, but you can see extraordinarily well in darkness. Am I right?"

Dead on, Slade thought.

"Tell me something, Detective. How did you explain your...affliction to your colleagues. Haven't they ever wondered why you wear the glasses, why you insist on working at night?''

Slade hesitated a moment, then thought, what the hell? Traymore had already put most of the story together on his own anyway. ''My personnel file contains the name of a very rare disease which makes eyes sensitive to light. There's a scientific term for it, one very hard to pronounce. There were questions at first, but I did my job and people finally stopped asking.''

''I see,'' Traymore said.

''Now *you* tell *me* something,'' Slade said. ''What do you plan to do with these conclusions of yours?''

The old man shrugged. ''Why, nothing at all, Detective. I'm here to help you.''

''I don't need your help,'' Slade said.

''Don't you? You see, I've also put together another conclusion. What if D'Angelo didn't die in that fire? What if he's the one responsible for all these killings? What if he and Roman Gerard are one and the same?''

It was a conclusion that had been simmering at the fringes of Slade's own mind for days now, but he'd tried to deny it. What if Drake D'Angelo *had* somehow risen from the ashes of death to seek his revenge against Slade? What better way than to kill the women Slade had warned away from the darkness? To make a mockery of the Mission that Slade had helped to found? To take away the one decent thing he still had left in his life?

What if Slade once again had to face an enemy eminently more powerful than any who had come after him? Would he have the willpower to resist the cunning of a monster who had honed his evil for over five hundred years?

Would he be able to defeat him this time? Or would it be Slade who succumbed instead? Would it be Slade who took that last, irreparable step into the darkness?

"I saw him burn," Slade said. "I saw both of them burn."

"Did you see his ashes?"

Slade shook his head. "I blacked out. I'm not even sure how I made it outside. But his clothes were on fire. His flesh was melting away. There's no way he could have survived that."

"Vampires are remarkably resilient," Traymore said. "They can lie underground for years, even centuries, while massive wounds heal. Then they rise again, ravenous for blood and often hungry for revenge. In D'Angelo's eyes, you killed Simone. You destroyed the woman he had chosen for his mate. What better way than to take something—or someone—from you?"

Like a deadly wind, fear swept through Slade. It wasn't the Mission D'Angelo wanted to destroy. Not anymore. He'd found a more effective revenge. He'd found something that would torment Slade as nothing else would. "Erin," he whispered.

"Exactly. From here on in, Detective, you will have to be very, very careful. The closer *you* become to Erin Ramsey, the more D'Angelo will want *her*."

Slade had only been gone a few minutes when the phone rang. Erin stared at the telephone for a moment wondering if she should answer it or let the machine pick up. Then, realizing that it might be Nick, she jerked up the receiver. "Hello?"

"Erin. Thank God I found you."

Erin frowned at the voice. "Racine? How in the world did you know I was here? How did you get this number?"

"It wasn't easy, believe me. Are you alone?"

"Yes. What's the matter?" A feeling of dread slipped over her.

"I can't tell you on the phone. I have to see you in person. I'll come pick you up." Racine's voice sounded excited. "You won't believe what I've found out. I think I know who killed Megan."

Erin's heart turned over. "My God, what are you saying?"

"It's true. I have so much to tell you. And show you. I can be there in fifteen minutes. Meet me outside."

"Racine, wait." But the phone had already gone dead. Erin replaced the receiver, then sat staring at the phone for a full half minute before she finally jumped into action. Racine knew who killed Megan? Could it be true? Could Erin's mission finally be over?

An uneasiness swept over her, but even though her heart pounded in fear, Erin started to get dressed. Her fingers were shaking as she buttoned her blouse, and for a long moment she debated on whether or not to leave Nick a note. She scribbled a brief message that told him she was going to meet Racine, then hastily scrawled her name across the bottom. Without looking back, she hurried outside to wait for Racine.

Erin stood shivering at the curb as she waited. It was still dark outside. Dawn was at least an hour away, and the street was deserted, eerily silent. Steam rose from the sidewalk grates and mingled with the early morning mist. A gust of wind stirred trash in the gutter, and an aluminum can clanged along the alley behind her. Erin jumped, glancing over her shoulder.

Finally, Erin spotted headlights coming down the street, and a car swished to a halt beside the curb. Racine leaned across the front seat and opened the passenger door. "Get in," she said urgently. "Hurry!"

Erin slid inside and closed the door, then turned to face Racine. The redhead's face looked as pale as a ghost's in the dim light from the dash. But her eyes glittered like emeralds, and her hair blazed as if it were on fire, making her seem almost ethereal, no longer a part of this world. Wordlessly she shifted the car into drive and pulled out into the street.

"You said you know who killed Megan," Erin said without preamble. "Tell me everything."

Racine slanted her a brief glance, then checked the rearview mirror. "Never mind all that now. I have to show you something first. Then you'll know, too."

"Racine—"

"In a few minutes you'll know everything. Trust me." Racine spared her another glance. "You look pale, Erin. Are you okay?"

"I'm a little cold," Erin admitted. She shivered uncontrollably. It was freezing inside the car. Evidently Racine's heater was on the blink, or else she'd forgotten to turn it on. Erin huddled inside her coat, but she still felt chilled by the damp. Racine, on the other hand, appeared oblivious to the cold. She wore a filmy black dress with a long silk scarf wrapped elegantly around her neck. She threw Erin an enigmatic look. Erin began to grow uneasy. Racine seemed so different tonight. So secretive. "How did you find out where Nick lives?" she asked suddenly.

Racine smiled. "I found one of his cards in the hallway. He must have dropped it."

Erin frowned in the darkness. The card he'd given her didn't have his home address on it. Did it? She tried to remember, but Racine cut into her thoughts.

"I've learned a lot more about your Detective

Slade," Racine said. "He killed someone, Erin. Did you know that? He killed his fiancée."

"It was an accident," Erin said quickly.

"Was it? The investigation was dropped, but he was never really cleared. And now all these women are turning up dead. Women *he* knew."

"How do you know about that?"

"I saw him with Megan, remember?"

"Yes, but what about the others?"

"What about them? They used to go to that club. The papers said so."

Had that information been in the papers? Erin tried to recall the articles she'd read, but it was so cold in the car it was difficult to think. She hugged her coat more tightly around her.

They had been steadily driving away from the river, and now Racine turned down the street toward the apartment building. She whipped the car to the curb and killed the engine. Erin looked around.

"No one's about at this hour," Racine said as if reading Erin's thoughts.

"What are we doing here?" Erin's heart started to pound an uneasy rhythm.

Racine smiled. "Let's go in. You're really going to find this interesting. I knew all along there was something strange about Detective Slade."

They got out of the car and Racine hurried around to take Erin's arm. Her grip seemed abnormally strong. Erin glanced down and saw Racine's bloodred nails gleam against her white coat.

"Come on," Racine urged. "Don't you want to know the truth about him?"

"What truth? Racine, please tell me what you know."

"You look worried, Erin. You suspect him yourself, don't you? You already have your doubts about him. Admit it."

As if sensing Erin's inner turmoil, Racine propelled her inside, and the door closed behind them, shutting off the remnants of light that had filtered in from the street. The corridors and stairs lay in complete darkness.

A new tremor of fear shot through Erin. "Why aren't the lights on?"

"Power must be out. Don't worry. I have candles." Racine guided her toward the steps that led down to the basement apartment, but Erin hung back. "I can't go down there."

"Of course you can." Racine's grip on her arm tightened. "Don't you want to know the truth, Erin? The whole truth about Megan? And Detective Slade? Think about it. Why have you never seen him in daylight? Why does he always wear those dark glasses?"

"This is crazy," Erin said again, but her mind was flashing so rapidly with images she felt light-headed. Nick, his eyes hidden by dark glasses. His face pale in the moonlight, but somehow extraordinarily alive.

The black leather coat that blended with the night around him. And his own words, "I belong to the night, Erin, and nothing will ever change that."

The first time she'd seen him, Erin had thought how one with the night he seemed, how very much a part of the darkness he appeared. And she had never seen him in sunlight....

Erin swayed against the wall. "He can't be," she protested weakly. "I would have known."

"But you *have* known, Erin. You just haven't wanted to believe it. Think about it. Why did he lie to you about knowing Megan? Why did he try to keep you away from the investigation? Because he was afraid of what you might find out about *him* if you stayed around asking questions."

Erin closed her eyes briefly. Racine wasn't telling her anything she hadn't wondered herself. The doubts, the suspicions...they had been there all along.

"You know what I'm saying makes sense, don't you?" Racine was leading her down the steps toward the basement. "He's been doing everything in his power to keep you away from the investigation. Now he's trying another tactic. He's trying to get you to trust him. Has he succeeded, Erin? Do you trust him?"

"I...don't know," she admitted.

"Do you trust him enough to leave here without learning the truth?" Racine demanded. "Can you live with that? Is your faith in him that great? If you can answer yes to those questions, then turn around, Erin. Run away. I won't try to stop you. Run back to *him*...and take your chances.''

Racine's voice was like a chisel, chipping away at Erin's faith, not just in Nick, but in herself. Had she been wrong to trust him? All these years she'd protected herself, built up her defenses, but Nick had penetrated those walls so easily. He had made her believe what she had so desperately wanted to believe. But she had to know the truth now. No matter what it cost her.

"Show me," she whispered.

Racine's white teeth flashed in the darkness as she grinned in triumph. "I knew it! Your faith *isn't* strong enough. Come on," she urged. "It's down here."

"But why here?" Erin asked when they reached the bottom of the stairs. They paused outside the basement apartment, and Erin's heart began to pound even harder. Behind that door lay her greatest fears. After all these years, did she dare face the monsters?

"There's nothing to be afraid of," Racine prompted, her eyes gleaming. She shoved open the door and stepped inside. "We're quite alone."

Moonlight filtered in through a high window as Erin stepped inside the apartment. She heard a sound, a muffled little cry that sent chills scurrying up her spine. "What's that?"

Racine shrugged. "Rats probably. This building is very old. But then, you know that better than I, don't you?'' She lit another candle. In the eerie, flickering glow, her eyes looked almost red and her hair seemed to crackle with an unholy fire.

Erin rubbed her arms, feeling increasingly chilled as she gazed around. ''What did you want to show me?'' she asked.

''I'll be right back.'' Racine opened another door and disappeared inside.

Erin walked around the room. It was almost empty, except for a huge wooden crate shoved against one wall. It looked as if some kind of appliance might have been delivered in it. A refrigerator, perhaps. There was nothing inside the room that seemed the least bit threatening.

Erin took a deep breath and began to relax. But as she stepped closer to the crate, she heard the smothered cry again. She knelt and peered in the shadows behind the box. A cat huddled against it, shivering from cold and fear. It wasn't the same cat she'd seen the other night, and Erin thought how odd it was that another one would be down here. Automatically she reached for the animal. The cat sniffed her hand, then meowed again, this time as if begging her to rescue it.

''Come here,'' she said softly. ''I won't hurt you.'' Gently she lifted the cat from its hiding place, and cuddled it against her coat.

''Where did you find that cat?''

Racine's voice startled Erin. She jumped, and her

grip tightened convulsively. The animal cried out in protest, its claws seeking purchase against Erin's bare hand.

"Ouch!" The sharp sting made Erin release her hold. The cat jumped from her arms and raced toward the door to the hallway, then vanished through the crack. Erin started to go after it.

"Don't bother," Racine said sharply. "He won't be needing it now."

"He? Who are you talking about?" Erin lifted her hand to examine the wound. It was almost in the exact same place the other scratch had been.

"Are you bleeding?" Racine asked quickly, almost hopefully, it seemed to Erin.

"Just barely. Who were you talking about, Racine?" Erin demanded.

"I think you already know."

"This is ridiculous. I'm tired of your riddles. Show me what you have to show me, and let's get out of here." Erin's uneasiness began to grow. "I really think I should go back to Nick's place. He'll be looking for me."

"He'll be occupied for hours."

"How do you know?"

"I just know. Trust me, Erin. By the time he finds you, it'll be too late."

Her voice sent a wave of chills through Erin. "Too late for what?"

"To stop you from finding out the truth. Look at

these pictures, Erin. Look at these pictures and tell me you think your Detective Slade isn't responsible for the killings.''

Racine opened the book she'd been holding and set it on the floor beside one of the candles. Then she backed away, motioning Erin to take a look. Reluctantly Erin knelt and gazed at the newspaper clippings and pictures mounted inside the scrapbook. They were all about Nick. She looked up. ''Where did you get this?''

''I've been doing a little research,'' she said evasively.

Erin turned back to the articles. There was a picture of Nick, taken as he left the hospital. His hands were heavily bandaged, his eyes already covered by dark glasses as he tried to look away from the cameras. The headline above the photo seemed to scream at her. POLICE OFFICER QUESTIONED IN FIANCÉE'S DEATH.

The article went on to describe Detective Slade's suspicious behavior, how he'd refused to answer questions even after he'd been suspended from the force. He'd hidden himself away in an old warehouse down by the river and refused to come out. If not for the commissioner's intervention, Slade surely would have faced criminal charges. Even after he'd been reinstated, the questions had remained and the rumors had continued to rage. Especially when it was learned he would only work at night.

''My God,'' Erin breathed. It all seemed so clear

to her now. She staggered to her feet. "I have to get out of here," she said numbly. But when she turned to ask Racine for help, Erin discovered that she was all alone. "Racine?" Her voice echoed back to haunt her in the empty apartment. Erin stumbled to the door, tried the knob and found it locked. She pounded on the wood. "Racine? What are you doing? Let me out!"

But again, the only answer she got was the sound of her own voice vibrating eerily off the walls. Trying to quell her rising panic, she hurried across the room to the other door Racine had opened earlier, but the knob rattled uselessly in her hand.

Erin turned, gazed up at the window that was beyond her reach and realized that she was trapped inside the basement where the monsters of her childhood had once lived.

# CHAPTER FIFTEEN

*The closer you become to Erin Ramsey, the more D'Angelo will want her.*

Dr. Traymore's warning rang in Slade's head as he sped through the darkened streets, trying to get back to Erin. She was safe, he tried to convince himself. He'd taken the necessary precautions in his apartment. No one, not even a vampire as powerful as D'Angelo, could enter Slade's private domain.

Still, he found himself running red lights, ignoring speed limits as he rushed through the deserted streets. What a damned fool he was to think for even a moment that he could ever have someone like her. His past would always come between them. The darkness would always be there to threaten them.

Slade would never find peace. He knew that now. Not as long as the evil that was D'Angelo existed in the world. He would never reach the light because from now on he would have to go deeper and deeper into the darkness to find his enemy, to destroy Drake D'Angelo once and for all.

He loved Erin. He knew that now. He loved her, but he couldn't have her, he thought with a pain that went deeper than any he'd ever before experienced. His love would only destroy her. All he could do now was send her away from him, as far and as fast as he could.

He pulled into the warehouse and shut off the engine, getting out and walking to the elevator. He barely registered the ride. When the metal cage stopped, he slid up the elevator door and strode into his apartment. "Erin?"

The silence that answered him was like a scream.

"Erin!" He ran through the apartment into the bedroom. Her clothes were gone. The only thing left to indicate she'd ever been there was the rumpled bed that gave silent testimony to their passion a few hours ago and the subtle, misty fragrance of lilacs that clung to the air like a haunting memory. As Slade stood there in the doorway, the scent seemed to fade as if Erin herself was now beyond his reach.

Then he saw her note and realized why she had left the apartment. She had been lured outside where nothing could protect her. A dark rage more powerful than any he'd experienced before swept over him. Erin was gone from him. She was out there somewhere in the night, and a monster who wanted nothing more than revenge against Slade was stalking her.

D'Angelo.

It could be no other.

The name rose before Slade like a black wave of evil. Deep inside, he'd always known that he and D'Angelo would meet again, that the final outcome of their destiny had not yet been determined. He had always known that there would have to be a final resolution to the conflict.

But this time, there would be no mistakes. This time, one of them would have to die.

Slade turned and walked out the door without looking back.

Erin slid down the wall and sat on the floor, her eyes glued to the shadows moving outside the window. She could see the moon crowning the treetops, and for just a moment, something blocked the lunar light. It looked like the silhouette of a huge, winged creature—a bat, perhaps. Then the shadow swooped down toward the window. Erin's hand flew to her face as if for protection. When she dared look again, the silhouette of a woman was standing just outside the window.

"I'm cold, Erin. So cold. Open the window and let me come in."

Erin blinked, trying to dissolve the image in front of her that had spoken in her sister's voice. "No," she cried. "You're not real."

"Help me, sissy." The figure lifted one arm and beckoned to Erin, a supplication so powerful that Erin found herself rising against her will. Slowly she walked toward the window.

"I'm dreaming," she said out loud, refusing to believe what was happening.

The figure shook her head, and the dark hair rippled

with moonlight. "I've come back for you, sissy. Now we can be together. Open the window and let me come in."

"Megan." Erin whispered the name as tears rolled down her cheeks. She was scared, terrified beyond anything she'd ever experienced before, but beneath the fear was a hope so powerful it threatened to engulf her. To see Megan one more time. To have the chance to tell her sister how much she loved her. To beg Megan's forgiveness for leaving her... "How?" she asked, moving even closer to the window. "How can it be you?"

"I'll show you," Megan said, her voice flowing through the glass like the darkest of winds. "I'll show you everything. We can be together forever, Erin. Just open the window and let me come inside."

*"And whatever you do, don't invite anyone inside."*

Nick's warning reverberated through her soul. Erin shivered, holding back. "I...can't," she said. "It's too high. I can't reach it."

"Then come out here to me," Megan said. "Please hurry. I'm so scared. Help me, sissy. Please help me." Suddenly the figure before her was not the Megan who had died a few days ago, but the little girl who had begged Erin to save her from the monsters years and years ago. And she was crying, pleading with Erin to help her. "They're coming for me, Erin. Please come get me."

"I can't," she whispered, her voice broken, her heart thundering in confusion and fear. "The doors are locked. I'm trapped, Megan."

"Try them again," the voice pleaded, an iron thread running through it. "Hurry!"

Erin ran across the room, but before she could even try the knob, the door opened before her. Erin's steps faltered. Alarm pounded inside her. She looked back at the window.

"Hurry!" Megan urged again. Then a shadow appeared behind her, a looming silhouette that made her scream. "Hurry, sissy. He's here. He's come to get me."

Without thinking, Erin ran out the door and up the basement steps. She had to find Megan. She had to save her. She had to prove to her sister that she hadn't deserted her.

Erin dragged open the back door. A cold, damp wind whipped her hair against her cheek. As if from a distance, she heard Megan calling, "Don't leave me, Erin. Never again."

"I won't," Erin promised breathlessly. She hurried out into the backyard, where she had found Megan's body just a few nights ago. It was cold outside. So very cold, Erin thought as she peered through the night. "Megan?"

"Over here." Then Erin saw her. She was wearing a flowing white gown that shimmered with moonlight as her arms reached out to Erin in supplication. Her hair, as dark as night, flowed down her back. She smiled. "I've been waiting for you, Erin."

The voice sounded a little different now. Erin took a step toward her. "Megan? Is that you?"

The figure moved closer. She stepped from the shadows into the moonlight, and then Erin saw that the woman who stood before her wasn't Megan. It was Racine.

"You," Erin whispered. "It's been you all along. You made me believe Megan had come back, that she still needed me."

"I made you believe what you wanted to believe," Racine said, smiling.

"Why?"

"Because he wanted me to. Because he commanded it," she said. "Because he wanted you to come to him."

"Who? Are you saying that Nick—"

Racine's gaze lifted skyward. She was staring at the moon. A shadow drifted over her face, and she closed her eyes, shuddering in ecstasy. "He's here," she whispered.

Erin whirled, searching the darkness. A fierce wind rushed over her, tearing at her hair and clothes now in earnest, almost knocking her off her feet. She heard a laugh, a low, triumphant sound that vibrated with evil.

Slowly she turned toward the voice. A man stood in front of her, looking directly at her with eyes that glowed silver in the darkness. With eyes that were ringed with fire. Erin caught her breath, and he smiled. His fangs glistened in the moonlight. How had she ever thought him handsome? Erin wondered. He looked like a beast. The very embodiment of evil. He was dressed completely in black, his dark hair pulled back from his face.

"I've been waiting for you, Erin," said Roman Gerard.

"You're a monster," she said. "You killed my sister."

Gerard laughed. The fire in his eyes grew more brilliant. Erin tried to look away but found she couldn't. She was mesmerized—trapped by the power of his gaze. "Detective Slade killed your sister, Erin."

Erin's hand crawled to her throat. She could hardly breathe. "I don't believe you," she said.

"It's true. He killed Megan just as he did Simone. He tore out her heart, Erin."

Erin's head reeled. She felt sick. She didn't want to listen to Gerard anymore, but she had no choice. His voice kept her captive, made her listen. Made her believe… "Why?" she cried out.

"To destroy her chance for eternal life." Gerard was edging closer to her. Erin wanted to run. She sensed his power, and it terrified her, but she could do nothing to save herself. She couldn't move, couldn't scream. Could only stand there held by his eyes and hypnotized by that satiny voice.

"Racine," she pleaded, "please help me."

"She can't help you," Gerard said. "She's under my power. When I've finished with you, I'll take care of her. And then Slade will take the blame."

"Why do you hate him so?"

The fire flashed in his eyes. "He took from me the one thing I loved most in this world," he roared. "He took Simone. And now I'll take from him. I'll take and take and take until he has nothing left." In the blink of an eye, one hand whipped out and he seized the back of Erin's neck. Effortlessly he drew her to him, forcing her gaze upward to his eyes. "See me," he commanded. "Know my power."

"No!" But the treacherous lethargy had slipped over her again. No matter how hard she tried, Erin couldn't look away. She stared deep into those glowing depths and a thousand images rushed through her mind. She saw Megan and Desiree standing together, calling to her, beckoning her to join them. She would never have to be alone again.

"I can give you that, Erin." The beguiling voice slid over her, shattering her defenses. "I can give you your darkest fantasies. Your deepest desires. Close your eyes and see it all."

Erin struggled to keep her eyes open, but her lids were suddenly so heavy she couldn't fight the languor. Her eyes drifted closed as Gerard's mouth moved toward her neck. "Nick!" she cried, in a last bid for sanity. "Help me!"

"No one can help you now," Gerard said.

Erin felt little more than a sting at first, then the pain at her neck deepened. She screamed and tried to push him away, but his arms were like steel. He held her against him, sinking his fangs into her throat, drinking her blood until she grew so weak that the pain began ebbing and the pleasure surged.

"Erin!" She was dimly aware of a voice calling to her through the darkness.

"Nick." She murmured his name but she had neither the will nor the strength to resist Gerard's kiss. The pleasure deepened and she strained toward him craving more.

"Erin, no!"

Gerard's mouth lifted from her neck and the pleasure began to fade. Erin became aware of the pain again. She reached for Gerard, trying to draw him back, but he released her and Erin crumpled to the ground.

Slade had never known such fear as he did the moment he saw Erin fall. With the last vestige of control he could muster, he willed himself not to rush to her. He had to be smart. He couldn't let down his guard, even for a second.

"Is she dead?" He tried to keep his voice even, emotionless, giving D'Angelo no hint of his true feelings.

D'Angelo smiled. "There's dead and then there's *dead*." His fangs gleamed in the moonlight. There was blood on his mouth. Erin's blood. Slade's insides twisted at the sight. "Don't try to pretend you don't care about her, Slade. I've seen you with her. I've heard the way she calls your name."

"She means nothing to me."

"Then you won't mind if I finish what I started." D'Angelo moved toward Erin. In a flash, Slade moved between them. D'Angelo's eyes glowed. "You move quickly for a mortal, Slade. I must give you credit. But you're no match for me. You never have been. You took Simone from me, and now you will have to pay."

"You're the one who destroyed Simone," Slade said. "You turned her into a monster as vile as you are."

D'Angelo threw back his head and roared with laughter. The sound echoed in the night like thunder. "You still don't understand, do you? *She* came to *me*. She *wanted* what I could give her. She craved the darkness."

"You're lying. You seduced her. You put her under a spell—"

"Simone was worthy of so much more than you could possibly imagine. You could never appreciate someone like her."

An image of Simone flashed through Slade's mind. He saw her beautiful face, saw her beguiling smile, but he realized now that there had always been something else in her eyes. A coldness that he had tried to ignore. For the first time since she'd died, Slade let himself see Simone for the woman she really was. A woman who had chosen darkness over light. A woman who had chosen death over life. A woman he couldn't have saved no matter what he might have done.

The guilt he had lived with for so many years began to lift from his shoulders. Slade stared at D'Angelo, knowing he could defeat him now. No longer chained to the past, he had faith in himself once more.

"You killed Simone," D'Angelo said again. "And for that I shall rip out your heart. But first, I want you to see what I've done to your precious Erin." He knelt and tilted Erin's head. In the moonlight, Slade saw two thin trickles of blood oozing down her neck. "She's mine now," D'Angelo taunted. "For eternity."

"I'll see you in hell first," Slade snarled. He had a stake in his pocket and he reached for it as D'Angelo began to circle him. "Erin," Slade called tersely, willing her to open her eyes, to get up and run to safety. But she lay on the ground motionless, while the blood continued to run down her neck.

"I can make this painless," D'Angelo taunted, "or excruciating. Guess which one I've chosen for you." He moved in then, anxious for the kill. Slade drew back his stake, but D'Angelo reached out, and in a heartbeat, snatched it and flung it to the ground, laughing. "What's a vampire hunter without his stake? Let's see what you can do against me now."

His movements were no more than a blur as he flung out his hand. Slade felt the breath leave him in a rush as he flew through the darkness and landed against the side of the wrought-iron fence that enclosed the backyard. Every bone in his body seemed to be snapping as he lay where he'd fallen, stunned. He got up and faced D'Angelo again. And again the vampire sent him sailing. Time after time, Slade got up only to have D'Angelo knock him away, as if he were no more harmless than a fly.

He was going about this all wrong, Slade thought groggily. Shaking his head to clear it, he ignored the cold smile D'Angelo directed toward him as he patiently waited to knock him senseless again. Slade was playing by D'Angelo's rules. He had to be smarter, think faster. He had to put the knowledge he had gained over the past eight years to use. He had to be cunning, diabolical, evil. He had to think like D'Angelo.

D'Angelo stood over him, grinning, his fangs dripping. "I could finish you off just like that," he said, snapping his fingers. "But what pleasure would there be in that? So much more satisfying to let you know what I have planned for the charming Erin. I'll drink from her again, Slade. I'll drink my fill while you lie there and watch helplessly. She's mine now, and there's nothing you can do to stop me.''

He had to find a weapon, Slade thought desperately, and almost immediately he saw it. One of the metal spikes in the fence had come loose and lay several feet away. If he could reach it before D'Angelo saw him, he might have a chance. Erin might have a chance.

He stretched out his arm, reaching for the spike. It was just out of his reach. If he tried to get up, D'Angelo would see him, stop him. Then there would be no hope for Erin.

He struggled again to reach the spike. D'Angelo was standing over Erin now, gazing down at her. His eyes were glowing, eager for more blood.

Slade moved an inch, but he still couldn't reach the spike. Desperation filled him. Then something moved in the shadows just beyond where Slade lay. Racine, her face pale in the moonlight, her hair blazing like fire, slowly bent down and reached for the spike. For a moment, Slade thought this was the end. There was no hope left. Then miraculously, she tossed the spike toward Slade and he caught it, rolling to his feet in one quick motion.

D'Angelo looked up. His eyes widened. But it was too late.

With all his might, Slade hurled the spike through the darkness, straight toward D'Angelo's heart. The vampire flew backward from the force as the spike drove through him. He struggled to his knees and looked first at the stake through his heart, then at Slade. His expression was one of cold black fury, of disbelief. Blood poured out of the wound and stained his chest in ever-widening circles. Though his hands struggled with the iron spike, his strength had already diminished far too much to allow him to remove it.

"You fool," he said, looking up, eyes blazing with a mad gleam. "You can't defeat me." But already the skin that had been flooded with his blood was decaying, turning to ashes before Slade's eyes.

Disgusted and sickened, Slade turned from the sight and hurried to Erin, taking her in his arms. She lay limp, pale and lifeless, unresponsive to his touch. "Erin! Can you hear me?" Dear God, it couldn't be over. He couldn't be too late to save her....

A voice spoke in the darkness, and instinctively Slade's arms tightened around Erin. "Get her inside," Traymore said urgently. "Hurry. It's almost dawn. The sunlight could kill her. I'll take care of Racine. She's merely hypnotized, I think."

Gently Slade picked Erin up, cradling her in his arms as he carried her into the building and up the stairs to her apartment. For a moment, his gaze lit on the roses she'd bought a few days ago. Already they had wilted, and now he understood.

D'Angelo could have taken her at any time. She didn't have to invite him inside. He'd already been in. The withered roses he'd seen the night Megan had died should have told him that. But he hadn't known then who he was dealing with.

D'Angelo could easily have taken Erin at any time, but instead he'd waited. Waited until Slade had fallen in love with her. Waited until the pain of her loss would be unbearable. And now, even in death, D'Angelo was still exacting his revenge.

"Put her down on the bed," Traymore said behind him. Slade did as he was told, and the old man bent over her, examining the puncture marks on her neck. "Downstairs in my apartment," he said over his shoulder, "there's a book on my desk. You'll know it when you see it."

"Can you save her?" Slade questioned hoarsely. "Is it too late?"

"I don't know," Dr. Traymore said. "Go get the book. Quickly!"

Slade rushed out, then came back, carrying the book gingerly. It was so old some of the pages were hardly more than dust. Dr. Traymore carefully took it from him.

"There are certain incantations in here. Prayers that we can try."

"No amount of hocus-pocus will help Erin now," Slade said angrily. "I thought you had a medicine. A cure, you said."

"This is all we've got," Dr. Traymore said. "You better muster up a little faith, Detective, if we're to have any chance at all. If anyone can help her, it's you. Talk to her. Let her know she has a choice. Let her know that there is a way out of the darkness. It's called love, Detective. Show her the way.''

The darkness was complete, but Erin wasn't afraid. The night welcomed her. She heard Megan's voice and knew she wasn't alone anymore. But she couldn't find her sister in the darkness. There seemed to be two paths ahead of her, and Erin didn't know which way to go. One was dark and one was light. Megan spoke to her out of the shadows.

''I've been waiting for you, Erin. Now we can be together forever. You want that, don't you?''

''Yes.'' More than anything she wanted to see her sister again.

''Then come to me,'' Megan whispered. ''Make the choice, Erin.''

Without thinking, Erin started toward her sister's voice. But another voice was speaking to her now, speaking to her from the path with the light. ''Come back to me, Erin. I need you. I...love you. Please, Erin. Can you hear me?''

''Nick?'' Her heart surged with joy. ''You love me?''

''Yes. More than anything. Come back to me, Erin.''

Erin turned back to the dark path. She could still see her sister in the shadows, but Megan's form was wavering now, dissolving like mist. ''You've found your way and I've found mine," she said. "Goodbye, Erin."

"Goodbye, Megan," she breathed sadly.

She opened her eyes and saw Nick.

He was sitting on the edge of her bed, clutching her hand in his. He was no longer wearing the dark glasses, and his eyes—so light and clear and beautiful—were staring down at her with so much love, so much faith that Erin could have wept.

"You came back," he whispered.

"I heard you calling to me," she said softly, lifting his scarred hand to her face. "I heard you say that—"

"I love you? I do," he said. "More than anything."

Erin had never known such joy. Her smile was radiant, full of light. "I love you, too, Nick. I have from the moment I first saw you." It wasn't his darkness that had drawn her, Erin realized now. It wasn't her fear of him that had so intrigued her. It was his strength. It was his faith that good could triumph over evil.

Deep inside, she had always known that he was the one man who could rescue her from the nightmares. He was the one man who could lead her out of the darkness of her past. And he had.

He lifted her up and carried her to the window. It was still dark outside, but in the distance the sky had lightened.

"What about your eyes?" she asked. "Shouldn't you cover them?"

"In a minute," he said. But Erin didn't want to take any more chances. Tenderly, she slipped his glasses on him.

And then he kissed her as dawn burst upon the horizon.

\* \* \* \* \*

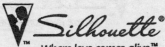